SREEPURAM SERIES BOOK 5

PREETHI VENUGOPALA

Contents

Contents

Such a love
That when it came
It blackened the rest
Of what I thought love to be
I was burned
Became ash
My ashes were scattered
And disappeared
But when they found your essence
My ashes came back
And formed into thousands
Of shapes again.
-Rumi

1

Navneet

July 23, Wayanad, 2019

One month. One month to relive old memories and make new ones.

When *Ammamma*, our dear grandmother had asked if we could plan for a month-long get-together for the Sreepuram family, it hadn't seemed like something we could pull off.

Our gang of cousins shared a strong bond right from childhood thanks to the many summer holidays we had spent together at Sreepuram. Time, however, had put a dampener on the fun times we desperately craved. We met when someone among us got married or if there was some other important family function. But the time we spent together hardly felt enough. So, after months of planning, we finally succeeded in carving out a month for ourselves. A month to be with the ones we loved the most.

What worked in our favour was that, of late, the majority of our Sreepuram gang had become entrepreneurs. We were our own bosses now. Even Kishore, who preferred working for reputed companies, had started a construction management company in the UAE and was raking in millions.

For me, it had taken a lot of effort to plan this month as my app development company, Quarks Info Solutions was a hugely successful multinational corporation. I couldn't take a month off but planned to work remotely. My business partner Rohit Varma, who was also my classmate and a close friend, helped me plan my monthly schedule to carve out enough family time each day.

Once we arrived at *Sree Nilayam*, Ammamma's home in Sreepuram, she had been the happiest. She played along with all our requests and promised to accompany us on the small trips we planned around the countryside. She spent time pampering us the way she always did. After all, we were her favourite humans on earth, though the new generation, the kids of her grandchildren, were slowly climbing the ranks.

Ammamma was to turn 75 in September but her enthusiasm outranked ours at any moment.

A blissful week passed in a jiffy. During the first week, we spent the days at Sreepuram, recreating carefree times and soaking in Ammamma's love. In the second week, we moved to a picturesque resort nestled amidst the green, misty mountains of Wayanad.

The decision to move to the resort was taken unanimously because we wanted to give a break to all the ladies in the family who insisted on taking over the burden of feeding and clothing us. Even with extra hired help, it had become exhausting for them at Sreepuram. Here at the resort, they weren't in charge of food, laundry or any of the other mundane stuff. The glow on their faces was proof enough that the decision had been a wise one.

We planned to stay there for a week before returning to Sreepuram and then proceed to Bangalore from where we would say our goodbyes.

If this reunion was proving one thing to me, it was that nothing could beat family love.

Over the years, the Sreepuram family had grown. Except for me, all my cousins were now married. Kishore, Ananya and Vishal were already parents. Kishore was the father of sixteen-year-old Aditya. Ananya had two very active primary schoolers Aryan and Ankit. Vishal had become a father recently to a cute, chubby little girl called Varada.

Compared to the others, I didn't even have a social life. Becoming the newest tech billionaire in India had come with its set of responsibilities. I didn't even have the energy to date anyone these days. I envied the kind of love my cousins shared with their spouses. Their love was endearing and hence watching them reminded me at times that something valuable was missing from my life.

"Do you think they found their soul-mates?" I asked Ammamma, gesturing at the happy faces of my cousins as we sat watching an impromptu hip-hop dance performance by Aditya in the common meeting area of the resort.

"Yes, of course," said Ammamma, as she massaged my hair with warm, herb-scented coconut oil.

I sighed with pleasure, as my scalp relaxed under the ministrations of her gentle fingers. Sitting in front of her like this brought back so many memories. Getting a head massage from Ammamma used to be one of the highlights of every summer vacation in my childhood. There was something inexplicably sweet about the experience. Our conversations during the activity would always be filled with bulb-on moments as my grandmother was a very wise woman. She always had answers to our many questions.

Even now, in this age of technology, her words made total sense.

"Do you think I will find mine too?" I asked, just to keep the conversation going.

"Of course. I have a feeling that you will find your special someone soon," she said, continuing to massage my scalp in circles.

"How will I know if that someone is my soulmate?"

"You will just know. Trust me, the moment you realize that the person in front of you is your soulmate, the emotions you feel will be inexplicable, incomparable and even overwhelming. No one will be able to erase or replicate the feelings your soulmate will evoke in you. You will find solace only in her," said Ammamma.

I had, once, experienced something vaguely akin to what she was describing. Nothing as magnificent though; maybe a minuscule of that. When I realized it was a one-sided affair, I mourned and whined for a week and then went back to my former carefree life. It hadn't hurt. But the experience had killed the urge to fall in love ever again. I didn't feel the need to love or be loved anymore. I'd decided love wasn't meant for me.

True love according to my brother Naveen was like a boomerang. Even if you threw it away, it returned to you. It had, in his case. But I had seen how much he had struggled until reuniting with his long-lost love, Arya. Somehow, I doubted whether I could live through something like that.

"What if I meet my soulmate and fate separated us?" I asked, thinking about all the heartache my brother Naveen had gone through before getting united with his soulmate. The guilt that I had played a role, unknowingly, in separating them years ago had been an unexpected shock. It had made me wary about falling in love. It had convinced me that when it came to matters of the heart, I was a fool.

"Destiny might play its own game, but true love always finds a way. Loveless life isn't worth living. So be open to receiving. The universe will never keep you from your lover if she is indeed the one for you," Ammamma explained.

"Ammamma, stop wasting your energy. There is no use talking to him about love. He is married to his company. Please ask him to go and take a bath. We want to start for the trek immediately after lunch," said Naveen, as he walked by us carrying Varada. Addressing me, he said, "I will kick your ass if I see you here when I return."

I showed him my middle finger. He retorted by mouthing curses.

"Go and take bath before he comes back," said Ammamma with a pat on my cheeks.

I got up, stretched my body and returned to my room to bathe and get ready for the trek. Today, the men in our group were going for a trek whereas the women planned to spend a day at the spa followed by a movie night. Some of the resort's trained staff had been hired for babysitting the kids and engaging them in various recreational activities.

Right after we reached Wayanad, Vishal suggested that we trek to a nearby peak called Neelimala. According to him, the Neelimala viewpoint was a magical one. But the women hadn't been so keen when he recounted the amount of trekking involved. Hence we had made separate plans. Vishal, being an avid trekker, had already been there a few times and knew the route quite well. Hence, he became our team leader by default.

We left the resort at about two in the afternoon, reached the base camp hotel at around three and began the trek immediately. As expected, the trek proved to be an enthralling experience. The hills with their dense greens and exquisite scents awakened our senses. Humour and easy camaraderie among the gang added a zing at every step. Even though we were dead tired and wind-beaten by the time we reached the summit of the peak, it was totally worth it.

"Ah, so this is what heaven looks like," exclaimed Arjun, once we reached the top.

There was hardly anyone else at the summit other than us. It felt like our personal paradise. The vista was unlike any I had ever seen. Inhaling the fresh air deeply, I took in the blue sky on the horizon, the white fluffy clouds below us and the Meenmutty waterfall in the distance. The fragrance, the birdsong, the sound of cascading water, the fresh air... it was an exhilarating kaleidoscope of treats for the senses.

Just as I sat down on the green grass to savour the moment fully, my mobile started screaming.

"What the hell! Whose mobile is destroying heaven's peace? Turn it off before I toss it down to hell," hollered Vishal.

It was a reminder alarm I'd set two days ago.

"Call Mr Mike at 4:45 PM," it said. I cringed. Mike was one of our VIP clients. He was one of my first clients when I started and he preferred to work directly with me. He was with me through my initial ups and down, and had trusted a newbie like me with many high-end projects. I couldn't miss this call.

When I'd scheduled the call, I had been at the resort where we had good cell phone reception. Now, I was in the middle of nowhere with no mobile coverage whatsoever. Then I remembered that a kilometre or so downhill, I had seen Arjun and Naveen making calls.

I had hardly ten minutes to get to that place. The uphill trek had been difficult from there and had taken us about thirty minutes. Downhill couldn't be that hard, could it? Of course not!

"Guys, I need to make a quick call. I'll be back soon. It's very urgent," I said. As I rushed down the slope, I tried to tune out the shouts of 'You are a loser,' 'Forget it and come back right now,' from my brothers. But I couldn't because they were so loud!

I'd almost forgotten that I wasn't allowed to just forget about my job anymore. Now I had responsibilities. The livelihoods of thousands of my employees depended on me. I raced downhill, concentrating on finding a network connection, winding in and out of paths we had traversed while going up. Just when I was about to give up, two signal bars appeared on my mobile screen.

I dialled Mr Mike's number and we talked. The call went on roughly for about half an hour. Mr Mike conveyed he liked all our ideas and I cleared whatever doubts he had about our proposal. We ended the call with Mr Mike agreeing to send the signed contract for his new project — one that was worth a million dollars —by the next day morning.

All was well. With a victorious grin, I looked around. I was surrounded by tall eucalyptus trees. For a moment, nothing seemed alarming. Then reality struck.

This region looked completely unfamiliar. Thanks to my habit of walking around while talking on the phone, I didn't remember when or how I had entered this Eucalyptus plantation. The path we had walked before had looked well-trod. The path I was standing on appeared relatively untrodden. I walked back to a nearby clearing and tried to find the way I'd come down from the summit. In my hurry, I hadn't even noticed the direction I had taken while running down random paths. All I could see now were rows and rows of Eucalyptus trees. The landscape looked the same in every direction. Where had the mud road that wound through a tea plantation and led to the summit vanished?

After wandering about for more than half an hour, I came to the crippling conclusion that I was probably walking in circles. Without losing hope, I hollered the names of Vishal, Naveen, Arjun and Kishore. No one answered.

I continued wandering for yet another hour without getting anywhere near any possible path to human inhabitation. They would be coming down now, wouldn't they? And they would be surely worried. I should have marked my way at least. Stupid, stupid me!

The sun was slowly setting behind the hills and darkness was spreading like a thick blanket. I panicked remembering all the instructions the forest guides at the base camp had given us before allowing us into the area.

"Come down from the peak before the sun sets. All kinds of wild animals come out when it is dark. There are occasional wildfires too."

Around me, the tall trees stood mocking my predicament. All I had was my phone and my wallet. I had a thin jacket on but it wouldn't be of much help as the night temperatures here in the hills sometimes dropped closer to zero. I hadn't even taken my backpack with me as I ran downhill.

"Is anyone here?" I cried out, hoping to hear from someone. Nothing again.

Fearful scenarios of being eaten by a tiger, trampled by a tusker and freezing to death began to slowly make rounds inside my head. I stopped, took a deep breath and listened to the sounds of the forest. As of now, nothing seemed alarming. I could hear the gentle tweets of the birds, the distant melody of flowing water and the wind whispering as it rustled with the tree branches.

I should have downloaded the Google map of the area. As I had been scampering around, I was now no longer in the area with the network coverage. I was never good at hiking like the others. My direction sense was pathetic.

I reached a place surrounded by huge boulders and decided to rest for a while. My throat was parched and my stomach was rumbling. Was there fresh water somewhere near? We had crossed a stream while going uphill with clear and fresh water. Which direction was it? Inhaling a deep lungful of fresh air, I endeavoured to calm myself and relax my body by doing *pranayama*. Ten minutes of breathwork infused me with energy and soothed my fears. As I ended the breathing exercise, I heard a soft strain of music floating toward me from somewhere near. Not just any music but Justin Beiber screaming *Despacito*.

I was not a fan of the guy's music but this time I welcomed his song with gratitude. Following the music, I walked blindly across the hill. It was growing louder by the minute and I finally identified the source of the music.

On the apex of the hill, I was on, I could see a building. Was it a resort? I hoped it was.

A mud path through the wilderness wound towards the building and I set upon it. It took me another ten minutes to walk there. By then, Justin's song had given way to the latest Bollywood hits. Up close, the building didn't look large enough to be a resort. It was an old British-style bungalow, definitely someone's home.

The visual that greeted me as I entered the bungalow's compound made me pause and gape.

In the middle of the yard, a bonfire was burning bright and a girl was dancing around it, swaying to the music oblivious of anyone or anything around. She was dancing as if she couldn't stop her body from moving, as if the music was ingrained in her being and she had to move to remain sane.

I stood transfixed, admiring her dance moves, the beauty of her loose curls that glowed like flames in the firelight and her enticing curves. She was dressed in one of those full-length dresses that girls preferred wearing these days. The dress was white with black polka dots on it and hugged her curves like a second skin.

The music was streaming from a stereo kept on the verandah. The modern music and the rustic surroundings clashed but she seemed to be the merging point for both. Her dressing was modern but she looked every inch like a daughter of these hills. Pure and exotic.

Who was she? Was she a hallucination caused by my exhaustion? Or was I dreaming? I raised my mobile and quietly clicked a pic. I knew I shouldn't but I needed proof to reassure myself that this was real.

I checked the photo and zoomed in on her face. My heart skipped a beat. She was beautiful. Doe eyes, skin that shone like alabaster and a riot of curls that framed her heart-shaped face. Something sharp pierced right through my heart.

Hers was the kind of face that poets would write sonnets on. Or the face nations might go to war for. There wasn't a spot of makeup on her face except for the kohl lining her eyes. She looked like some untouched, enchanted forest bloom. In the wilderness, she stood out bright like a blazing fire.

Just when I thought nothing could beat this vision, Mark Anthony's 'You sang to me' started playing. The girl stood still for a few moments and then started whirling. Her dress billowed around her resembling the tunic of a whirling dervish dancer. Thanks to her, two different universes —Mark Anthony's heartfelt singing and the cosmic dance of the dervishes —merged effortlessly right in front of my eyes, uplifting my soul and captivating my senses.

I knew then that I would never forget this moment till the end of my life. Nor would I be able to forget this girl.

2

Aathira

When the song ended, I sat down on the verandah and took deep breaths to calm down my tired body and wretched heart. I emptied the contents of the box next to me into the fire and watched ten years of my naive dreams burn. I sat down and poked the items around to make them burn properly.

The song changed to a peppy number and when I danced again, I stepped on my dress and stumbled but caught myself before I fell. Why had I even bothered to dress up this way? Unlike my usual attire of jeans and *kurti*, I had shopped for a dress in the latest fashion and had worn it to impress my crush, Pratik.

After all, he used to always nag me to dress like a woman. I had thought that today would be the day, the day he would propose to me after ten long years of being close friends. How naive had I been!

In my head, today would have been the day that I would describe to my kids and grandkids.

"It was on a cold, windy afternoon that he proposed to me." I had even written the entire script in my head. Pathetic.

I kicked a pebble lying on the ground with all the anger I felt. Pain shot up through my toes. It wasn't a pebble, but the tip of a big rock. Was the universe deliberately messing up with me today? Anger rushed right up my toes and spread to the tip of my curls.

I picked another song to dance —*Shake it off* by Shakira.

Was there a way to delete every single memory associated with that bastard who had played with my heart for a decade? I wished I could skin him alive. I wished I could slowly roast him after marinating him for hours in a mixture of barbecue sauce, garam masala and ginger-garlic paste.

But why was I blaming him alone? This wouldn't have happened if I hadn't been so blind.

I poked the logs in the fire with anger and watched as the sparks flew high.

A part of me grieved as I watched my old journals burn. But a part of me felt relieved. I had devoted hours poring down my thoughts in those pages that were being consumed by the flames. I had spent hours creating scrapbooks using photos, movie tickets, chocolate wrappers and whatnot. I had amassed years' worth of memorabilia associated with that scoundrel. I had been nothing but a besotted fool.

There had been red flags right from the beginning and I had ignored all of them. I had shrugged off the warnings from everyone. I had ignored the words of my besties, my gang of friends, the STAR quartet. They had always discouraged me from following Pratik around like a smitten puppy.

My argument had been that they didn't know Pratik as much as I did. After being schoolmates for more than six years, God had ended up putting us in the same engineering college, that too for the same course. They had known Pratik only for four years, but I had been friends with him for years and secretly in love with him from the very beginning.

I hadn't checked our WhatsApp group after posting a photo of me all dressed up and declaring my intention to go and confess my feelings to Pratik. As I knew they would dissuade me, I'd switched off the broadband connection immediately and hadn't turned it back on. It was time I talked to them. I went inside the house and turned the WiFi on.

Messages started piling up one after the other. Mostly, the notifications were from the STAR Quartet. I opened Whatsapp and read their messages.

Trisha: Don't do it. Get your eyesight checked. I wonder what you see in him.

Sneha: He has made her wear those dark glasses that make people go blind. I want to slap that idiot Pratik.

Riddhi: One day she will rue how she ignored all our advice and fell for that idiot.

Trisha: What happened? Did you do it?

Sneha: Answer, girl. We are dying here.

Riddhi: What's wrong with your landline? I tried calling. Says all lines to the route are busy. Why do you live at the edge of the earth?

Trisha: Message us, you idiot.

All the messages after that were of them calling me names and saying they would oust me from the group. Threats, pleas and also jokes about how horrible it would be if Pratik became my boyfriend. The last message was sent a few minutes ago.

I decided to respond.

Me: Girls, relax. I didn't confess to Pratik. I was kidding. I went to a wedding reception. You guys are so naive.

Within seconds, happy emojis began to flood the group.

Me: Guys, got to go. Mom will kill me if I sit tapping on the phone. Will message tomorrow morning, okay? Miss me.

Trisha: Yo, you girl from the hills... Good night then. *Saranghae!*

Saranghae? It took me a few seconds to recall that it meant 'I love you' in Korean. That had been the first Korean word Trisha had taught me. Thank God I didn't ask what she meant by that. She would gobble me up for forgetting.

Riddhi: Goodnight sweetum.

Sneha: Check your mail early tomorrow. The results of our campus interview will be out tomorrow. Sleep tight, goodnight!

Me: Okay!

God, I missed them. They would be doing a happy dance here if they knew what had happened. Each one would say to my face, "I told you so."

Yup, they had repeatedly told me to stop obsessing over Pratik. Right from the beginning of our first semester of engineering, when I had confessed to them about my crush.

I couldn't wait to see them again. But would we ever be together again the way we had been these past four years? If it all went as we hoped, we would.

The campus interview had gone well for all four of us. We just hoped we would all get selected. The company we had applied to was owned by a former alumnus of our college whose start-up had become a global name overnight when a wealthy American angel investor had decided to back it. The company had become our first choice as they were keen on taking in newbies, especially from our college.

What fun it would be to work at an MNC with my besties. The company had its headquarters in Bangalore and we would have to move there.

The other three of the STAR Quartet —Sneha Nair, Trisha George, and Riddhi Singh —belonged to well-off families. Riddhi, especially, was an heiress and didn't really need a job. But she wished to be independent and couldn't wait to start earning herself. My case was different. I needed this job desperately.

All my life, my brain had been my ticket to a good life. I had been a rank holder in my 10th and 12th board exams and had gotten into a good engineering college with a high rank and scholarship. If I hadn't, I might have joined the labour force of the tea plantation here, like my parents.

The landline rang shaking me out of my reverie. I picked up the phone after clearing my throat a few times.

"Aathira, I think we won't be able to return home tonight. I am so sorry darling but you know how your father is acting these days. He started drinking and now he can barely walk. We will have to stay here. Will you be okay, sweetheart?"

It was my mother. I hadn't expected this.

My father was acting like a reckless man as he had hardly a month left to retire from his job as the assistant manager of this tea estate. Within a month, he would have to leave this house and these hills. He had started getting drunk daily after receiving his dismissal notice. No one ever stayed till the age of fifty-five as an assistant estate manager as he had. He loved these hills and the estate like his own. Just the thought of leaving it all behind was killing him.

Today's function was the wedding reception of his best friend's son. He had a legit reason to celebrate. He and his friends would most probably drink all night.

"Well, darling, your father is insisting that we return. No one here is sober. But he is bothered that you are all alone in that house with a bad lock in the middle of a jungle."

"It's okay, Amma. It's not like I am staying alone for the first time." I had stayed alone at night before on similar occasions for a few hours but never the whole night.

Anyway, I was the one who had decided to stay home and hence I had to deal with the consequences. After the fiasco that happened today evening, I wasn't ready to face anyone anyway. Especially at a wedding reception where the topics of discussion usually revolved around marriage, love and proposals.

"Let Sheru loose and close the main gate. We will return by around nine, okay?" Amma said.

"Okay. You go and get him to stop drinking. Tell him I want him to," I urged her.

I was worried about his health. He had developed diabetes recently and had suffered from high BP for a while now. Yet, he was least bothered about his well-being.

I kept the phone on its cradle and plodded to the backyard to get Sheru. As if our tiny mutt could protect me. He was the worst guard dog ever. At the first sign of trouble, he would tuck his tail between his leg and run off. The coward. But that didn't make him any less lovable. He was my little darling. He made me feel as if he loved me like I was his everything.

Sheru barked excitedly on seeing me. I hunkered down and unlocked his kennel. He dashed out and immediately began his happy dance. He ran around me in circles, jumped on me and licked my face until it was covered by his saliva. Then he lay on the ground and demanded a belly rub. I gave in to his request. The moment I stopped, he nudged me with his paw, urging me to continue.

"Get your butt off the ground right now and follow me. I didn't even close the main door. Do you understand? *Appa* and Amma are staying over at their friend's place tonight. That means you are in charge. Got it?"

As if he completely understood what I said, Sheru immediately got up and thrust his nose up into the air and wagged his tail. He seemed rather proud and determined to prove his worth.

I walked back into the house, closed the back door and returned to the front verandah accompanied by Sheru. Sheru began growling the moment I stepped into the front courtyard to gather my things and extinguish the fire.

"What is it, Sheru?" I asked looking in the direction in which he was glaring.

I saw the man at the same moment Sheru dashed towards him, barking his head off.

I could see a young man warming his hands in the bonfire. Who could it be? No one usually came this way other than our acquaintances or people from the estate. Our house was the only one for miles around. Was he some trekker who had lost his way and wandered into our courtyard? We got visitors like those once in a blue moon.

I was scared a bit but curious as well.

My little hero had taken off to confront the stranger and was now growling at him. Instead of getting intimidated, the young man who appeared to be in his late twenties or early thirties grinned at Sheru. He crouched down and held out his palm to Sheru. Clearly, he seemed like a dog lover. Sheru stopped barking, sniffed his palm and began to wag his tail. The stranger started petting him. And to my disgust, Sheru allowed him.

The traitor!

3

Navneet

The sweet mutt was now on his back and demanding a belly rub. With a chuckle, I complied. My gaze wandered to the owner of the dog.

She looked stunned or probably just surprised. Tall by Indian standards, she stood there as if analysing whether to fight or flee. Her riotous, fiery curls had now cascaded down her shoulders, covering her bosom and reaching her waist. My heart started thumping hard against my ribs in some intriguing ancient rhythm.

"Sheru, come to me right now!" she called out. I loved how melodious her voice sounded. It caused my racing heart to thump faster. Maybe she could sing too, not just dance like a dream.

Sheru looked conflicted. The poor guy even had his name weighing on him. Who named a cute little thing like him after the king of the forest? The girl called him again and he took off. Once he reached near her, he turned to me and barked. He was back in his protector mode again. I chuckled. The girl seemed wary. I waved at her to put her at ease and addressed her to find a solution to my problem.

"I am sorry for intruding this way. But I got lost in the hills and was separated from my fellow trekkers. I heard a telephone ringing. Can I use it to contact my team?"

She hesitated for a minute but then simply said, "Okay."

Shouldn't she be scared of letting a stranger into her home? Maybe this happened often in this area. Maybe I was not the first one who had gotten lost in these hills.

Instead of letting me into the house though, she asked me to wait. Then, asking Sheru to stay put at the main door, she went inside. After a few minutes, she arrived holding an old-fashioned rotary telephone. She connected it to the phone wire she had thrown out through the window that opened into the verandah. Once connected, she checked if it was working properly and then gestured at me to go ahead and use it.

I dialled Naveen's number and he picked up after a few rings.

"It's me. I got lost," I said immediately when he answered.

"Thank God. We were so worried and were about to contact the forest guides. Where are you now? Are you okay? We searched for you everywhere," asked Naveen.

"I am okay. Just exhausted. I am at a house in the hills."

"That's good. Just stay there tonight. We will come and get you in the morning, okay?" he said.

"I am not so sure if I can do that. Isn't there any way that you can come and get me now?"

"Ask them if you can stay the night. If not, ask them if they can help you get to the main road or provide some vehicle."

I covered the mouthpiece of the phone and addressed the girl.

"Can you give me directions to the town?"

"We use a shortcut through the jungle usually to get to town. But it won't be safe during the night unless you are travelling in a group. I am sorry, but I don't think I can help," she said.

"Is there a place nearby where I can stay tonight?" I asked, just hoping that the people here would allow me to stay.

She didn't answer for a long minute. Then she looked around as if considering her options.

"You can stay in our outhouse. My father has gone out and once he returns, he will help you get to town," she said.

"Wonderful. Thank you so much," I said, smiling at her.

I removed my hand from the mouthpiece of the phone and told Naveen that I had a place to stay the night. Thus, having sorted things out, I kept the handset back in its cradle.

Without another word, she disconnected the phone, threw the wire back through the window and went inside to restore it to its original place.

I looked around. There were a few cardboard boxes on the verandah filled with books. Most of them looked like diaries. From the looks of it, these books were being fed to the fire. I sat on the edge of the verandah and immediately, Sheru came and lay near me. He was gazing at me fondly as if we had been friends since birth. I extended my hand toward him and immediately he was on his back expecting a good belly rub. How cute!

"Sheru, you are such a disappointment," said the girl as she came out of the house. Sheru ignored her completely and prodded me with his paw when I stopped giving him belly rubs.

"Don't be so harsh on the poor fellow. He is such a darling. How old is he?" I asked.

"Two years old," she said. "Sheru doesn't get close with strangers this fast. Are you some dog-whisperer or something?"

"I wish! I am just a techie," I said.

"Ah, I am one too. I should say, I will be a techie once I start a job."

I wanted to ask her where she had graduated from but maybe I shouldn't. I was intruding into her home and I didn't want to invade her privacy as well.

"In Bangalore, where I work, they have this joke. If you throw a stone into the sky in Bangalore, it would either land on a stray dog or a techie," I said to lighten the mood.

She laughed. I liked the sound of it. I liked how her eyes sparkled when she smiled. I loved the charm of her straight, pearly white teeth. Her soft, petal-like lips made my gaze linger on them a bit longer than necessary and I looked away quickly to maintain decency.

"Can I have some water? I got separated from my gang hours ago and I walked for miles I think," I said.

"Sure," she said and went inside to fetch water.

She returned after a minute and handed me a glass of warm water. It felt like an elixir after being thirsty for hours.

"You seem exhausted. Are you okay eating non-veg?" she asked.

"Oh, I eat anything that doesn't bite me back," I said. Just at the mention of food, my stomach began to rumble.

"Okay. Let me get something for you to eat. Just give me a minute," she said. Before she went in, she emptied the contents of one cardboard box into the fire and stirred the ember with a bamboo rod. The fire began burning bright once again. Warmth enveloped me like a cocoon.

She went inside the house leaving me alone in Sheru's company. I caressed his ears and he sighed with contentment.

"So champ, is it true you don't behave like this with strangers?" I asked Sheru and he answered with a short bark, which almost sounded like a 'yup' to me.

"Then okay. Else, people might think you are not a good guard dog," I said. Sheru responded with a long moan.

"No, no. You are not bad at all. You did scare me when you first sprang at me. You really lived up to your name then. You see, I love dogs and hence seeing you made me happy." This time, Sheru's response was a low-pitched moan.

"By the way, don't you think you are a little too tiny for a two-year-old?" Sheru sighed.

"You should eat well, pal! Aren't your humans feeding you well?" Sheru barked twice. I took that as a yes.

"Maybe your father or your mother was a Pomeranian. If that is the case, you won't grow much. This is it. But I tell you, you look good. Let no one tell you otherwise."

Sheru groaned. He lay beside me and pawed me again demanding that I continue with the belly rub.

I obeyed.

I asked him more questions and he made appropriate sounds, making me feel as if we were having a real conversation. I was liking this little mutt even more with every passing minute. I wondered what was delaying his human.

My stomach was preparing to riot.

4

Aathira

I couldn't help but smile as I listened to the conversation happening outside between the stranger and Sheru. It was intriguing as I too often engaged in similar heart-to-heart conversations with him. Though Sheru wasn't the bravest among dogs, he never took to strangers the way he did to this man.

I didn't even know his name. Yet, here I was, preparing to feed him and allowing him to sleep under my roof. Like Sheru, I had begun to trust him too.

When he had asked me if he could stay the night, I hadn't had the heart to say no. He looked exhausted and lonely. It was a norm at our home to give shelter to people who were stranded in the hills. But at those times, Appa would be the one offering them shelter. Even though I was alone at home, I felt I shouldn't say no to this stranger. For some inexplicable reason, I felt safe around him. There was something about him that made me want to know him better.

It was not because he was handsome. Maybe that factor did influence me. He had a memorable, clean-shaven face with the hint of a day-old stubble, thick eyebrows and very expressive eyes. He was about six feet tall, with broad shoulders and an athletic build. Someone who could play the role of a hero in an action movie. When he looked at you, you wanted to believe every single word he was uttering. Maybe it was his aura that made me want him to stay. Or it was simply because I was craving company. I didn't want to be alone tonight.

If someone saw me now, they would conclude I had lost my mind. Standing in the living room, carrying this dinner tray loaded with food and eavesdropping on a stranger's conversation with my dog was nothing like my normal behaviour. Then again, nothing about today could be considered usual. I was a wreck within after the rosy glass through which I viewed the world had shattered. After dancing around the bonfire of my battered dreams, I had begun to see what the others had been saying all along.

It hurt to accept that I had been living in an illusion for as long as I could remember. I had been filling in the blanks in my own story, compensating for things that it lacked with my fertile imagination. I'd given significance to words and situations that meant nothing in reality.

Sheru's sharp barks stopped my wool-gathering. He was standing on the verandah facing me and barking his head off. He was questioning why the hell I was standing inside carrying the food tray instead of handing it over to his starving new friend.

I glared at him and then walked into the verandah as if I had just walked out then from the kitchen. I kept the dinner tray on the small coffee table on the verandah and handed a brass tumbler with water to my guest.

"Please use this water to wash your hands," I said. Though we had a garden pipe, it was common courtesy in our household to give fresh water in a brass tumbler to visitors to wash their hands before food.

I watched furtively as he walked to the border of the courtyard and washed his hands and face with the water in the tumbler. I handed him a cloth napkin to wipe his hands once he returned.

"Mmm. Something smells good," he said looking at the food.

Amma had made egg curry in a gravy enriched with coconut milk, *uppumanga chammandhi* (a side dish for rice made with shredded coconut, pickled mango and chillies) and potato *mezhukkupuratti* (Kerala-style potato stir fry). All three were my favourite dishes. She had prepared them as I was missing out on all the yummy food at the reception.

"It will taste good as well. My mother is an excellent cook," I said. "You eat. I'll be back."

After locking the main door from inside and leaving Sheru in the stranger's company, I returned to my room and took a quick shower. With all that mindless dancing, my body felt dirty. I was feeling awkward even standing in front of my guest. I must be looking like a vagabond. After washing away the grime and sweat, I dabbed a bit of moisturizer over my face and then changed into a cotton churidar that I wore at home. I took a fresh bed sheet, a bath towel, some other bathroom essentials, track pants and a T-shirt from my father's cupboard and headed to the outhouse.

Our outhouse was more like a small single BHK home. This was where unexpected guests to the tea estate stayed back in those days when my house used to be the estate manager's home. About five years ago, the tea company had built a bigger, modern house for the estate manager and the old building was allotted to my father, the assistant manager.

My father had started at the estate as a tea picker some twenty years ago and had slowly climbed the ranks.

By the end of the current month, this house wouldn't remain ours anymore. It was sad as this place held so many memories.

These past years, the outhouse had become my haven whenever I needed to get away from the noise and craziness of my family. My father loved to keep the television on full-time even if no one was watching. It was the constant background music in our home. I would stock the outhouse with my favourite books, and snacks and brew myself a coffee while I immersed myself in the world of books.

I loved reading romances. While reading all those books, in my head, Pratik and I always replaced the male and female leads. Did romances like those actually exist? I wasn't sure anymore.

I caught myself humming a tune as I changed the bed sheet and wondered where the sadness frothing inside me had vanished. Strangely, it felt like the dog-whisperer had murmured some mysterious mantra in my ears to cheer me up.

When I returned to the verandah, I found that my guest had finished his dinner and had washed the plate as well from the garden pipe. Had the food been enough? I had given him almost the same amount of rice I usually served my father.

"Thank your mother for that delicious food. She's got magic in her hands," he said upon noticing me.

"I will tell her. Let me show you to the outhouse. You seem tired."

"Thank you. Lead the way," he said. I flicked the light on in the path to the outhouse and guided him.

"I have kept a fresh towel in the bathroom. There is also a T-shirt and a pair of track pants if you wish to take a shower and change. The light in the bathroom doesn't work. So, I have kept a lit candle there. Call me if you need anything else," I said as I waved him into the guest house.

"I don't know how to thank you. Tell your mother I am truly grateful for this. I will personally thank her in the morning."

I realized I hadn't mentioned that my mother was away too. I didn't bother to change that. It was better this way. It was not because I thought he might pounce on me if he knew I was alone. But because triggered by the events of today afternoon, my faith in men as a whole was at an all-time low. When I hadn't been able to correctly judge the man I'd loved for a decade, how accurate would my assessment of this man's character be?

I bid him good night and returned to the courtyard to burn the rest of my journals. Ten years' worth of scribblings. I picked one from five years ago and flicked through it.

Pratik smiled at me right when he saw me on the way to school today. He slowed his cycle and talked to me till we reached school. We mainly talked about the topics that might be important for the unit test. I am so happy.

Pratik borrowed my English notebook and complimented me on my handwriting. My heart! English Ma'am asked me later why my essay was the same as Pratik's. I was slightly disappointed that he had copied my essay instead of using it as an inspiration. But it's okay. He has been so busy with his badminton practice this week. If not mine, whose essay could he copy?

Pratik borrowed hundred rupees from me today. I just hope he returns the money soon. Appa would be mad if he knows this month's allowance is all gone.

My journal entries sounded pathetic to me now. The girl who wrote these words had been head over heels in love with Pratik. He had been her everything. In her eyes, Pratik couldn't do anything wrong. But the girl who was reading them now knew how naive she had been. She now realized Pratik had used her naivety as much as he could.

These journals had been my treasures till today afternoon. I used to open random ones when I missed Pratik too much and drown myself in old memories. Now as I tossed them into the fire, my heart felt lighter. As the fire consumed them, I felt like I was witnessing the funeral of that starry-eyed girl.

A part of me mourned her death. My heart felt empty.

5

Navneet

The shower water was ice cold, yet refreshing. It washed away my exhaustion within seconds and kicked my senses wide awake. The fragrance of the herbal soap along with the soothing light of the candle and the rustic setting made the bathroom seem like it belonged in some Ayurvedic spa.

After changing into the track pants that were a bit short and the T-shirt that was a little tight, I walked around the outhouse inspecting it. It was tiny but cosy. Everything here had a feminine touch, including the floral curtains, the lace borders on the pillows and the pastel bed sheet. Maybe this was my dancing Goddess's personal haven.

There was a shelf in the bedroom filled with books. Most of them were romances but there were other genres as well. I couldn't help but smile when I found a copy of Ammamma's latest book on the self. What would the girl say if I told her that Arundhati Mukundan was my grandmother?

I picked *Angels and Demons* by Dan Brown, a book that I had heard a lot about, and settled on the bed to read myself to sleep. Just as the story got intriguing, the power went out and I was plunged into darkness. Cursing the electricity board, I kept the book on the bed and sat up.

Through the windows in the tiny hall beyond the bedroom, I could see the light from the bonfire. Wasn't it time she extinguished the fire? I walked towards the window and looked outside. The girl was still sitting there feeding the books to the bonfire. Standing in the darkness, I observed her. Yet again, her mesmerizing beauty captivated me. But she looked despondent. As if she was dying inside. I checked my watch. It was nearly ten.

Why was she still up?

Most importantly why was she sad? Who had made her cry?

Curious, I opened the outhouse door and stepped outside.

She noticed me only when I was a few steps away from her.

"You startled me!" she gasped and exclaimed.

"Couldn't sleep. Saw you were still awake and thought of joining you. Why aren't you sleeping?" I asked.

"I will sleep after I burn these," she said, pointing at the last carton on the verandah.

"Is it urgent? Can't you do it tomorrow?" I urged her.

"No. It has to be done today. I might change my mind overnight and hang on to them like precious diamonds," she said tossing a few more diaries into the fire.

"If you don't mind me asking, what exactly are you burning?" I asked, curious as to why she was losing sleep to burn a carton of books.

"Remnants of the biggest mistake I made," she said and then looked away. I could sense the sadness in her voice. Maybe these were her journals.

Was it heartbreak?

Who in the world had given her so much sadness?

She had the face of an angel. No one in the right sense of their mind could hurt her intentionally. I felt anger surge within me against whoever had given her pain.

I didn't want to probe further though my mind was churning with questions.

Sheru came and sat near me. All three of us, sat there in companionable silence watching the embers. A spark from the fire shot up into the air and following its path, I looked up into the night sky. Never had I seen the night sky filled with so many stars. Up here in the mountains, the starry sky looked breathtaking, like a dark silk shawl studded with diamonds. I took a long breath and sighed.

When was the last time I paused to look at the stars?

When was the last time I felt this kind of peace?

The last year had been one mad rush. A year ago, an American billionaire bought one of my popular apps for a whopping 600 million dollars. I had shifted base to Bangalore and continued developing apps on demand. After having sold twenty more major apps within this short span, I was declared the newest billionaire in the startup world by popular business magazines.

The sudden growth had come with its own set of craziness. I had close to a thousand employees under me now and we were on a hiring spree as we weren't able to keep up with the demand. Nowadays, every coach and business owner wanted their own app. We were focusing on recruiting fresh engineering graduates as it was easy to mould youngsters to suit our needs than recruiting the sharks in the field who demanded higher salaries. The newbies usually required extensive training and we had a team to handle that.

This month's end, we had a fresh batch joining. Because of the Sreepuram family get-together, I'd handed over the entire responsibility of recruiting to Rohit.

Once the new batch was in place, the strain on our current staff was expected to significantly reduce. That meant breathing space for me as well.

That reminded me about the 10 AM conference call I had with the CEO of one of our VIP clients from the US.

"Will you guide me to the town early in the morning tomorrow? I have to be back in my hotel room by 10 AM."

"No problem. I will take you to the main road early in the morning tomorrow," she said.

"Thanks. By the way, I am Navneet," I said, offering a belated introduction.

"I am Aathira. Good to finally know your name," she said with a smile.

Aathira! The name suited her.

"Oh, so are you named after the star Thiruvathira of the Vedic system also known as the Ardra Nakshatra?" I asked.

"Yes. My mother is crazy about astrology. I was named Aathira as Thiruvathira is my birth star."

"Nice. My brother always talks about stars and destinies, and hence, I am deeply interested in the subject as well."

"I am not a believer but I have read Linda Goodman's Sun Signs and her descriptions are so eerily accurate."

"Is it? I haven't read it, so I can't comment. I started reading a Dan Brown book from your collection. *Angels and Demons.* Is it good?" I asked.

"Yup, it is. Almost as good as *The Da Vinci Code.* Have you read it?"

"No. But I've seen the movie," I confessed.

"Ha, the movie is nowhere as good as the book. Read the book."

"I am not much of a reader. Books put me to sleep. I am more of a movie buff," I told her frankly.

"I love movies too. But not as much as I love books. Most movie adaptations are disappointments. I prefer to create visuals in my mind as I read books. And they are always a lot better than the movie adaptations."

"I have heard that too. But I wonder why that happens. I mean now we have technology that can bring to screen anything that we can visualize. Why then do you think the movie adaptations fail to recreate the magic of the books on screen?"

I loved the sparkle in her eyes and the excitement in her voice when she talked about books. Probably, the best gift someone could give her was a book.

"I feel it is mostly because of the time restriction that reduces the level of detail you can explore in a movie. If a book is adapted into a drama series, it fairs better. We only need to compare the movie adaptations and drama series of Pride and Prejudice to know that," she said.

"I have watched the BBC drama version of Pride and Prejudice and the 2005 movie adaptation. Both were good. Again, I haven't read the book so can't comment on how close they were to the original story," I said.

I discovered them while spending time watching old English movies and dramas during an off-site posting in the UK in the early stages of my career.

"Both versions differ from the book in a lot of ways. But still, the BBC version kept the essence intact. The movie version lacked depth. And that happens mostly with all such adaptations," she said.

"The Harry Potter series was okay. I have read the books and they did keep the magic alive, I felt."

"Yes. But still, I prefer the Harry, Hermione and Ron in my head than their movie versions," she said, her eyes going all dreamy.

"Is it? I thought they were good enough. Especially in the first movie. They looked so cute."

"Yeah. They really set friendship goals. That is how friends should be."

"Do you have friends like that?" I asked, eager to know more about her.

"Yes. We call ourselves the STAR Quartet. An acronym created using the first letter of our names."

"A is you, who are the others?"

"S is Sneha, T is Trisha and R is Riddhi. We have been inseparable since day one of engineering."

"I have many friends but just one close friend. He is also a colleague now."

"Friends make everything seem better, don't you think? They are the only people who know our real self and love us unconditionally," she said.

"Yes. Friendship is so much better than love in my opinion. When in love we endeavour to impress our lover by trying to become the person they want us to be. And in the process, we often become so different from our true selves."

Aathira stared at me for a long minute and then said, "You seem to be speaking from experience."

I gazed at her. She was a stranger, yet somehow, I felt no qualms in telling her about the pain I had gone through. How that one single experience had burned me; how it had made me stay away from love ever since.

"You can say that. I have never been in love in the real sense. What I experienced was unrequited love. Years ago, I fell in love with a girl with the blindness and dogged determination of a first attachment. But she was in love with someone else. I was crushed when she got engaged to that person. And my heart never dared to love another again after that."

"Unrequited love sucks. Do you see these journals that I am burning? They once fueled my obsession with my crush. I noted down things like the colour of his shirt, the number of times he smiled at me, what we talked about, how handsome he looked and so much more. Ridiculous, right? When I reread them today, I understood what a pathetic fool I had been all these years. He had just been using me all the time. The truth was staring at me all the while, right from the pages of these journals. Right from page one. I tell you, you cannot find a girl as foolish as myself in the whole world."

My heart ached for her. I didn't know her story. I didn't know how the boy had used her or hurt her. But I could understand the place where she was currently. I was there once. It was a terrible place to be in. The pain of unrequited love retreated to a secret chamber in the heart and resurfaced once in a while to remind us to never fall in love again. It warned that love can break one's heart into a million pieces.

"Don't be so hard on yourself. I understand your grief. It hurts like hell to love in vain. When we love someone, we direct all our love to them. If they don't reciprocate, it feels like they have sucked out all the warm feelings from us. Like a river that freezes over in the absence of warmth, love becomes grief. Grief, as they say, is nothing but love with no place to go," I said, looking into her eyes, which by now, were pools of grief.

"I am grieving. Yes. But mostly for being so naive. For not understanding that I was wasting my time with him. My friends used to tell me to stop being so obsessed with him. But in my eyes, he was my best hope, my only chance at happiness."

I felt bad for her. "Do you know why they call it a 'crush'?" I said, making the air quotes gesture as I uttered the word crush.

"Why?"

"Because there is a 99.99% chance that your crush will just crush your ego, reject you and walk away."

She snorted, picked up a few more journals and tossed them into the fire and opened yet another carton.

"Let me help," I said and when she nodded, I picked up a notebook. "We had a life coaching session at our company last month where we were made to write our worst fears and regrets and then burn them. We had to tear the paper with all the anger we felt and drop the paper into the fire while repeating affirmations like '*I am letting go of all my anger and regret. Hey fire, take them*'. 'I am free' and so on. It felt silly initially but once we did it, it felt amazing."

"Let me try it then," she said and picked up another journal.

She tore the notebook and as she threw it, instead of an affirmation a curse flew out of her mouth.

"Go sucker, burn!" There was a gleam in her eyes as she watched the flames engulf the book. "Whoa, that feels so good."

She emptied the carton onto the verandah and picked another notebook.

I watched with amusement as she mixed her affirmations with curses as she hurled the notebooks into the fire with a renewed vigour.

What an endearing hellion she made!

My heart began to hum a love song, and I decided it was my cue to return to the outhouse. But I didn't want to go.

6

Aathira

Why wasn't it common knowledge that surrendering one's anger to fire was the best therapeutic tool ever? As I watched the journals burn, the anger simmering inside me diminished.

"I carried you in my heart for years. I am now free. I will no longer let you use me, you pea-brain," I yelled and threw another one of my journals into the fire.

Navneet laughed. He picked a notebook, tore it in half and gave it to me with a flourish. I accepted it with a bow and flung it into the fire shouting another affirmation-curse.

"Girl, you have such a fine collection of curses," said Navneet with a wide grin. My heart fluttered. Gosh, he looked so gorgeous. If Trisha was here, she would have gotten all the details of the guy including his great grandfather's first name.

"Thank you. Cursing him feels so good," I confessed.

"Now enough, okay? You've cursed him enough. My grandma says our curses find their way back to us. It adds to our negative karma or something similar."

"Oh, is it? Maybe I should stop cursing and stick to just the affirmations then."

"Yes, stick to the affirmations. Now repeat after me, 'I don't chase, I attract. The person who deserves me will find me.'"

It sounded very outlandish. Still, I picked up the last remaining notebook and threw it into the fire repeating the affirmation.

"I don't chase, I attract. The person who deserves me will find me."

Somehow that statement sounded incredulous even to my ears. I was no Goddess who had men falling at her feet begging for attention. No one even paused to give me a second look.

"Do these affirmations really work? They feel like fancy phrases to me," I said.

"According to our life coach, affirmations help to change the way we speak to ourselves. What were you telling yourself before this? Weren't you scolding yourself for believing this person? For wasting your time on him? For falling for him?"

"Yes, but that is natural, right?" I asked, wondering if anyone could think differently.

"And how did you feel after you scolded yourself? Miserable or relieved?"

"Miserable. I realized how pathetic I have been," I said softly.

"Exactly. And that leads to more heartache and self-pity. Instead, it helps if we become our best friends during difficult times. Changing the style we talk to ourselves using affirmations is the way to climb out of the pit of misery that we often fall into. When hurt, instead of scolding yourself, it helps if you give yourself a tight hug mentally and console yourself. It is necessary to tell ourselves that it is okay to make mistakes. It is okay to not be perfect. It is okay to be not okay. Instead of becoming your worst enemy, become your best friend. What would your best friends do if they were here now?"

"My friends will go and beat Pratik within an inch of his life. That's what they will do."

"You do have feisty friends. Pratik... So, that's his name, huh? Trust me, it's his loss entirely."

Navneet's eyes searched my face and I felt my cheeks heat up under the warmth of his gaze.

"What do you mean?" I asked.

"Are you fishing for compliments now?" Navneet flashed a smile, and my heart jiggled and wiggled.

"I am not. I am not a diva, nor am I an heiress like the girl he is currently going around with. He did not choose me. He chose her."

"His loss! Listen, someone will come along who will choose you without thinking twice. Trust me Aathira, you are beautiful. It's not because you are lacking in any way that he didn't choose you. People don't recognize the value of things that are there right under their noses. He is an idiot. And I would say good riddance."

I gazed into the fire because if I faced Navneet, he would see how much his words were affecting me. A sense of peace was washing over me. And that peace was kindling a different sort of light inside me. Of happiness.

"If it were you, would you choose me?" I asked, and thwacked myself mentally the moment the words left the tip of my tongue. What the hell was wrong with me?

Silence stood between us like a spooky stranger. Why did I ask such a stupid question?

"In a heartbeat...," Navneet said and our eyes duelled for a few long minutes.

Hearing his reply, my cheeks burned. Was it my imagination or did his gaze drop to my lips? My heart thudded wildly. I wished he was genuine and not saying what he said just for the sake of making me feel good. I kept staring at him, my eyes devouring him, summoning him to prove that he meant what he said.

Seconds passed and he just stood there, doing nothing even as the air around us crackled with some strange energy. Agonising seconds later, he stepped one step closer and then another until our bodies were mere inches apart. He inhaled sharply as he cupped my face.

"You have no idea what you're doing to me, " he whispered as he leaned his forehead against mine. I forgot to breathe when he stepped closer. He murmured my name as he kissed me over and over again. I revelled in pleasure as his hold tightened around me.

As his lips caused havoc and sent thrills thrumming through me, I bloomed like a rosebud, unfurling hidden layers of desire and discovering new pastures of pleasure. His tongue darted across my lower lip and pressed seeking entry. I gave in and was immediately sucked into a world of pleasure.

"You taste like heaven," he groaned when we stopped to breathe. His mouth landed on mine right the next minute with a ferocity that made my legs go weak. I threaded my fingers through his hair and moved closer. I quivered in his arms as his right hand wandered all over my back, roamed again and caressed the sides of my breasts. I hadn't ever known the kind of pleasure that shot through me as his thumbs grazed across my nipples over the many layers of my clothes.

I wondered how it would feel if he caressed my bare skin. As if in answer, his lips left mine and hopped down the pulse on my throat. When his lips touched the bare skin on my shoulders, every single cell in my body reacted as one. As if he was a magnet and they were iron filings, clinging to him for dear life.

He groaned and buried his face in my curls. He gathered me close, every hard contour of his body imprinting on mine. I let myself drown in his heat. When his lips returned to mine, I tried to return his kisses. I just did whatever he did to me. He nipped my lips with his teeth, and I did the same to him when I got the chance. He licked my lower lip, so I did the same to him when I could.

I stopped breathing when his rogue fingers caressed me, breathed when he paused. I don't know how long we kissed, but when we came up for a breath, my lips felt swollen and tender. I wanted more. But when he stepped closer and I felt his arousal, I realized where this could go. I wasn't ready for anything more. I didn't even know him. In every way, he was a stranger. Yet, I was allowing him liberties I had never allowed anyone.

What would he think of me?

A few minutes ago, I was whining about my unrequited love and now I was kissing him as if my life revolved around him. As if we were lovers.

This certainly couldn't be love. I had never known lust. Maybe this was just lust.

I pushed gently against his chest and moved away.

"I am sorry. This shouldn't have happened. I don't know what I was thinking. I apologize for my actions," I said.

Navneet looked taken aback for a moment. Then shaking his head, he stepped away from me.

"Please don't apologize. Don't take away the magic from this moment by saying you are sorry. I do not regret what happened. I am in awe of whatever this is that exists between us," he said, coming to a halt when he was a few metres away from me.

I shivered internally because the emotions he was evoking inside me were entirely new. I couldn't meet his eyes but my whole body longed to be back in his arms. I wanted to kiss him again, tremble in his arms as he made my body sing like a harp.

I wanted to be near him the whole night, talk to him, laugh with him and watch him smile at me. I was getting addicted to the way he looked at me. I don't remember anyone ever looking at me the way he did. Like I was his entire world. No one had made me feel the way he made me feel. But at the same time, I felt guilty. I felt terrible that my first kiss was with a total stranger. What had happened to my morals?

"I am ashamed of myself. In your eyes, I might look like someone who goes about having one-night stands with strangers. Just so that you know, that was my first kiss," I confessed, trying to right myself in his eyes.

"There is nothing to be ashamed of. We are adults and we shared a moment of passion. I assure you that I won't belittle you just because you allowed me to kiss you. I've been craving to kiss you from the moment I saw you. From the moment you appeared in front of me like this pagan goddess, dancing around the fire, making my heart flutter like a butterfly," he said.

I looked at him, refusing to believe him. Our eyes clashed and I felt that strong pull again. His words held magic. His warm gaze ignited a wildfire of longing within me.

If he had uttered another word and taken another step toward me, nothing would have stopped me from flying back into his arms. But silence reigned and we stood frozen for a few long moments as the bonfire behind us crackled and sputtered. The electricity chose that very moment to return, breaking the spell that was keeping me enthralled. Sheru woke up and barked sharply as if the bright light was annoying the hell out of him.

"You should go and sleep. I have to go in as well. Let's forget this happened. It won't do good to any of us," I said, turning away from him.

"Do you think I can forget this easily? I can't. I feel we were bound to meet like this. We are destined to be together," he said, stepping in front of me. His words sounded like the sweetest melody.

Could it be? Were we meant to be?

His eyes were sparkling with the intensity of his emotions. I sighed in defeat and let him pull me back into his arms. He let out a breath and pressed his forehead to mine. As desire began to cloud my vision, I shook my head and chided myself to be pragmatic. Every second in the company of this stranger was going to add fuel to the fire. Only I knew that I was all alone with him with no one around for miles.

What would he do if he knew my parents were away?

Would he drag me to bed and complete what we had begun?

"I think I hear my mother. She will go mad if she sees us together," I lied, gently pushing him away. "Do go and sleep. I will take you to the main road in the morning."

Navneet stood rooted to the spot as if he didn't want to go. Then he looked at the house, pivoted on his heels and walked away without another word.

As I watched him walk away, my chest constricted with an unknown pain.

7
Navneet

I dragged myself back to the outhouse even though I craved to turn back and gather her in my arms again. I didn't dally with girls. I had never been impulsive when it came to dating or love. Falling in love had not been a priority. My unrequited first love must have caused the apathy. That was the trouble with unrequited love. As there hadn't been a closure, it had lived within me undiminished forever.

Tonight, kissing Aathira made me realize three things.

First, I hadn't wanted it to end. Even now, I wanted to go back and claim her soft lips again.

Second, the girls I had kissed till now didn't hold a candle to Aathira.

The third and most important realization was that I was smitten. I didn't want to allow this connection between us to end the way it did.

In those brief minutes when she was in my arms, I had started dreaming about a future for us. Never did a kiss burn me from within like this. When I first touched her soft lips, I somehow knew in my bones that this girl was special.

I could never forget this. I wanted her beside me all my life. But the way she had dismissed our kiss, pained me. Did she want really want me to forget whatever had happened? I should try to convince her to give us a chance. With time, she would understand that I was earnest. My heart was screaming that she was mine and I wanted to believe it.

In the case of my first love, ninety per cent of everything that happened between us had occurred just inside my mind. I had interpreted all her actions and words differently only to realize later on how wrong I had been. We hadn't even kissed. She had been just a vivacious, good friend. That was all. Nothing more than a mirage.

With Aathira, the spark was kindled at the first sight. Without warning, this splendid girl had suddenly conquered my world and become my everything. I had always run from attachments and made excuses to not go on dates. Never had a warm body within the circle of my arms evoked the kind of desire that Aathira made me feel. The temptation to run to her, and steal another kiss was still raging inside me like a forest fire. I wanted to smell her again. A pleasant fragrance of wild flowers, like the very scent of the night on these hills.

Her taste still lingered on my lips. She tasted like hot chocolate on a cold winter morning. Warm, fragrant and soothing. My drab day had suddenly turned special, and every moment with her felt festive. I hadn't been able to stop tasting and had plundered her soft lips like a starved soul. It was no secret that I wanted to taste her again.

At the outhouse door, I paused and turned back to look at her one last time. She was no longer there in the front yard. I felt crushed. She must have poured water into the fire and doused it before making a hasty retreat. I looked at her door with longing.

What was she doing right now?

Was she thinking about me too?

She had apologized and called it a mistake. How could she?

I had never experienced something so delightful and unforgettable. In fact, this whole evening had been memorable. Right from the first moment I had seen her, dancing around the fire. Something strange had stabbed my gut then and my heart had started to race for no reason.

The little I knew about her now intrigued me. I wanted to know more about her. I wanted to hear her laughter. And selfishly, I wanted to be the reason she was happy.

I walked around the outhouse and imagined Aathira here. I could picture her studying for her exams right here, chewing her nails and wracking her brain with tough numerical problems.

I could picture her relaxing on the couch with a book and getting lost in the book's universe with a sparkle in her eyes.

She clearly believed in romance. Half her book shelf was filled with romances. I picked a book from the shelf. *The Notebook* by Nicholas Sparks. I hadn't read it but I didn't think I would be able to sleep after what had happened. Dan Brown and murder mysteries didn't spark my interest any longer. I had heard that Sparks' book was about the enduring power and miracles of love. I needed it to instil in myself the confidence that my love too stood a chance, even though, at the moment everything appeared bleak. I read the book till my eyes drooped shut sometime after midnight.

The next morning, birdsong and the sound of the morning breeze playing with the leaves woke me up. I glanced at my watch and saw that it was nearly eight. I had to get to town. But before that, I had to get Aathira's phone number. After changing out of the borrowed clothes from the previous night, I dressed quickly in my own clothes and walked to the main house. A light mist was still floating around the hills and I breathed in the fresh air with relish.

The enticing aroma of freshly brewed coffee greeted me as I approached her main door. I rang the bell and waited, praying that she would answer the door and not her mother.

My prayers were answered. Aathira greeted me with a shy smile but didn't raise her eyes to meet mine. She must have taken a shower. Her hair was a mass of soft curls on her shoulders that she had tied loosely with a tuft of her hair. She appeared fresh like dew. Pure and delectable. I felt the same stab in my gut again.

I longed to taste those lips. I longed to hug her.

"Come in and have some coffee. Then we can leave," she said.

Leave? I didn't want to leave. If I could, I'd stay here. With her. But my schedule for the day was crazy. I couldn't afford to act lousy just because I had fallen in love. I couldn't jeopardize my company's reputation by cancelling any of the scheduled meetings.

"Yes. Can we leave in fifteen minutes?" I asked, flashing a warm smile at her.

She nodded and invited me into the living room of her house. After directing me to the sofa, she went inside to fetch coffee. I searched if my phone had a signal inside the house. No. Luck definitely wasn't on my side.

Aathira's house was an old British-style bungalow. The living room even had a fireplace that seemed to be in use even today. There were framed photographs on the mantle. Happy family photos. Aathira with trophies and certificates. Aathira dancing. I loved how genuinely happy she looked in the photographs. I noticed she resembled her mother a lot. And she looked like she was her father's pet. In almost every photo, he had his arms forming a protective circle around her. I wished to meet them. I wished to be featured in one of such photos with them. Before I could go and look at the photos closely, I heard her footsteps.

Aathira came in with a steaming cup of coffee and a cheese sandwich.

"Sorry, I woke up late. This was all I could manage," she said. Why was she apologizing so often? It made me feel as if she still considered me a stranger. I was in no mood for her apologies. I wanted us to be close enough to banter. I wanted to tell her that I was mightily impressed by everything about her. I liked her, her home, the food that she had served—every single thing. All the little moments we had shared had already become etched in high definition inside my head.

"Where is your mother? I wish to thank her for her kind hospitality."

Aathira turned red.

"She is not here. My parents will return around nine only," she confessed, still not meeting my eyes.

"What? Were you all alone here yesterday night?" I asked, unable to believe it. I experienced a sharp pang of something that felt akin to betrayal. She hadn't trusted me with the truth that she had been alone. Had she been afraid of me?

"Not alone. I had Sheru. And trust me, I have spent many nights alone in this house without anything untoward happening. The hill is like a big brother. It protects us all."

I felt angry toward her parents. What if something had happened to her? What if someone with wrong intentions had come instead of me? The world could be a scary place. What if there had been a fire? How could her parents leave a beautiful girl like her alone at the mercy of chance? I had kissed her. Now I realized why she had used her mother as an excuse to get rid of me yesterday. She had been scared and alone.

Did she think I would have taken advantage of the absence of her parents if I had known it? Maybe yes.

"Where did they go? Why didn't you go with them?"

"They went to a wedding reception. I had some work to finish. And I am not really fond of going to parties, so...," she said.

"Promise me you will not stay alone like this ever again. At least, promise me, you will not welcome a stranger into your home when your parents are not around," I said, feeling suddenly concerned for her.

She stared at me for a long minute and then spoke.

"I never do. Somehow, you were an exception. And also, no one comes to these parts usually. This is like the middle of nowhere. No one can find this bungalow until they are right in front of it. We are well hidden and protected by nature. No road leads here as my father doesn't own a vehicle. There is only a small mud path, which is known to only the locals around here. And most of them were at the party yesterday."

"Okay, I'll stay here till they come," I said, looking out of the house, suddenly feeling anxious. Meetings could be rescheduled. I should stay here and protect her. In a way, it was a preposterous thought. Considering the kind of attraction I was still feeling towards her, at this moment, I posed the maximum threat to her.

Aathira was staring at me like she was convinced I had lost my mind. "Come on, don't be ridiculous. I have lived here for years. I am safe here than anywhere else on earth. And the few people who ended up in our courtyard were the nicest of people. And often, they come in groups. You are the first person who came in looking totally lost."

"Aha. So you took me in out of pity?" I asked. Why did it even matter?

"Of course. You looked like you might faint if I didn't let you in," she said.

I chuckled as she was so close to the truth. I had been almost at the end of my wits when I had seen her house. Feeling wretched and tired, I wandered into this courtyard and saw her dancing around the fire. From that moment on, it had turned into a charming, unforgettable adventure. If someone told me that some passing fairy or witch had sprinkled some magic dust on me and guided me towards this angel standing before me, I'd believe them.

Keeping my gaze focused on her face, I ate the sandwich. It tasted really good. I looked at her with admiration and the urge to kiss her returned with full force. My eyes searched her face to understand her state of mind. She was playing with a strand of her hair when our eyes met. My eyes quietly focused on her petal-soft lips. I watched, mesmerized, as they formed a perfect little heart as she blew out a breath. Every part of me hardened with desire. I wanted to pull her onto my lap and kiss her senseless. As if she could read my intentions, Aathira blushed and took a few steps away from me.

"I will be back in a second. You finish the coffee," she declared and dashed out of the living room, leaving me forlorn and disappointed.

8

Aathira

Lacing my fingers behind my head, I stood and watched the woods from my bedroom window, trying to delay going back into his presence for as long as I could. Those moments before I fled from the living room, were charged with something so powerful that it scared me. I had never felt such a trusting and intimate connection with anyone else. But I was scared. Scared of getting my heart broken. Scared of trusting this stranger who now no longer felt like one.

When I entered the living room again, Navneet looked up. He had finished eating the sandwich and was keeping back the empty coffee cup on the tray. Bathed in the morning light, he looked even more gorgeous than I remembered. My heart fluttered like a butterfly. When he caught me staring, I squirmed internally like a child caught red-handed doing something forbidden. He smiled. My heart! His gaze touched me like a soft caress and my chest began to rise and fall rapidly.

"Um, I think I forgot to lock the back door. Let me check. I will be back in a minute. You wait for me in the courtyard," I announced and took off again. Sitting on a kitchen stool, I took deep breaths, trying to calm myself down.

After unlocking the back door silently, I closed it with a bang just to ensure my lie didn't sound like one. Navneet was waiting for me in the front yard staring impatiently at his watch. My heart was still acting like it was high. Quietly, I put the collar and leash around Sheru, intending to take him along with us.

Sheru, who understood that I was taking him for a stroll, took off immediately like a rocket up the hill, dragging me along with him.

"Sheru, you little devil, not there. We have to go down the hill," I scolded as I dragged him back. Sheru whined and tried to pull me towards the woods where he usually found squirrels or rabbits to chase.

Navneet watched us, looking amused but didn't say anything. After finally directing Sheru to the small mud path that went downhill and joined the road that led to the town, I dared to look at Navneet again.

I wondered where he was from. How old was he? His clothes seemed expensive, as did his exquisite-looking watch with many dials. And his English had a slight foreign accent as if he had stayed abroad long enough to catch it.

"I really feel awful leaving you alone. I would've stayed till your parents came if I didn't have to attend an important conference call this morning," Navneet said. He sounded sincere.

"Stop worrying, will you? This is a part of life in the hills. Don't feel bad. They will be back by the time I return," I said trying to put him at ease.

"If you say so. I want you to know that I consider myself lucky that I got lost yesterday," he said. My heart! This was madness.

If I had known the reason for his sudden departure earlier, I would have perhaps offered to switch on our broadband connection that came with our landline. But no, that would have just given more time for the attraction I felt for him to grow. This was better. I should nip this, whatever it was, in the bud stage itself. I couldn't afford it to bloom and grow wings.

I was sure that he would forget all about me after a day or two. Even if he remembered, I'd just be a holiday fling. I didn't want to crave something that could never be mine.

Not again.

Navneet seemed to be lost in thoughts as well and both of us walked in silence for the next few minutes. When we reached the mud road that led to the town, Navneet suddenly turned to me.

"I recognize this road. So, I was this close to missing you, huh?" he said.

His choice of words warmed me. I didn't say anything but just smiled.

He pulled out his phone and cheered loudly when he found a network signal. He did something with great concentration and then flashed a very satisfied smile at me.

"Keep walking along this road for another hour and you will reach the town. If you are lucky, you might get a lift from one of the locals heading that way. See you then," I said, intending to get over with the inevitable goodbyes.

Navneet stopped browsing his phone and looked me straight in the eye.

"So, you are leaving?" he asked, wrinkling his eyebrows.

I nodded. What? Did he expect me to walk with him all the way to the town?

"Give me your phone number. I'll call you in the afternoon," he said.

"No need. We don't have network coverage at home anyway," I said.

"Then share your landline number," he demanded.

"No. I can't do that. I am not even going to tell my parents that I hosted a stranger at home yesterday night. I don't want any unnecessary complications," she said.

"Don't do this to me, Aathira. Did I offend you by taking liberties with you yesterday? I will apologize if I did. Please, don't shut me out of your life. Share your email ID at least. I feel like God connected us."

His words almost swayed me into sharing my email address. But I stopped myself at the last minute.

"If God connected us, don't you think we will meet again?" I countered.

"What if we meet again after years when you are already married and with kids? I don't want to even think about that," said Navneet.

"Wouldn't that mean God didn't want us to be together?" I asked. All the more reason that I shouldn't share any of my details with him, I thought.

Navneet looked at me for a long minute and then exhaled deeply.

"I am not giving up on us. I want you to know that you are special to me. Come what may, I will find a way back to you," he said, his eyes shining with determination.

My heart fluttered again. Was I making a mistake by letting him go? I had an impulse to tell him every single detail about my life, including the damn pin code of this place. But in the end, common sense prevailed.

He was a stranger. And a stranger he should remain. If not for anything, I had to do that for the sanity of my heart. Within a few mere hours in his presence, my heart was acting like a feisty, hormonal brat.

Navneet took a step toward me. "Please, Aathira. Let's keep in touch."

I shook my head and took a few steps back.

"This is it, then?" asked Navneet, hurt writ all over his face.

"Yes," I said aloud, though I sounded a bit loud and squeaky even to my own ears. My heart was protesting and my brain was short-circuiting.

Navneet looked defeated. He raked his hair with his fingers and then blew out a breath. He hunkered down to pet Sheru. Then he got up and faced me again.

"One last hug?" he asked as he approached me with steady steps. I nodded and allowed him to gather me in a hug. I let myself sink into his warmth one last time as he squeezed me tight.

"So, till we meet again," he whispered and stepped away. After taking a few steps, he returned to me and cupped my cheeks. His eyes were misty as he searched my face. Then with an aching gentleness, he kissed me. In a daze, I pressed myself against him and threaded my fingers through the hair on his nape. With a groan, he pulled me closer and sucked on my lower lip. I parted my lips, inviting him to explore my mouth. After a sensual assault that lasted several minutes, he abruptly stopped kissing me and moved away.

If he had turned back and approached me one more time, I would have fallen on my knees and begged him to continue kissing me. He had kissed me twice in a span of a few hours, and each time I was left longing for more. Tears pricked my eyes as I stared at his retreating back.

Fighting the urge to run toward him, I stood and watched, till he turned the bend in the road a few hundred meters ahead and vanished from my sight.

So, this was it. The end of my short but beautiful love story.

Yes, it was love.

It was after he left that I realized that he'd made me fall in love with him. The memory corner of last night was going to be the most visited part of my brain. I wished I had a photo to remember him by.

Sheru was barking his head off now because his new friend had left. I sat down on the ground and patted his head. He whined.

"I think loving someone or being loved by someone isn't written in my destiny, Sheru," I said as I hugged him. Sheru gave two sharp barks as if he didn't agree with my line of thought.

As seconds ticked past, the heaviness in my chest kept increasing. I wanted to run after Navneet and tell him that I too wished us to be together. That there could be a future for us if we really wanted.

But I didn't do or say anything. I was a coward. I wanted it but I wasn't brave enough to desire it or fight for it. And love was all about timing, wasn't it?

I had kicked away my chance, hadn't I?

If God wanted us to be together, wouldn't he bring us together again?

With that thought buzzing in my mind, I walked back home dragging a brooding Sheru.

9

Navneet

I kept walking trying to shake off the mountain of despair weighing on my heart. When the road took a sharp left turn, I felt the loss of the warmth of her gaze on me acutely. It was over. My brief foray into the realm of the heart had ended rather abruptly. I stopped as tears blurred my vision. I swiped away an errant tear drop and rubbed my chest to make the dull ache go away. The debilitating awareness that she didn't want to give us a chance kept nagging me. She had behaved as if yesterday's events were already in her forgettable past.

For me though, every thought, every breath and every cell in my being was pulsing with her name. She was my soulmate, my solace and my everything. And like Ammamma said, the emotions she had evoked in me were indeed inexplicable, incomparable and overwhelming. Those tiny sparks of love I'd felt when I first saw her had now transformed into an inferno.

After fighting the urge to go after her one more time, I resumed walking. This could wait. I had other responsibilities. I couldn't toss them away just because I was desperate to be with the girl I loved. I would return.

I would find her and make her fall in love with me as desperately as I had fallen in love with her. I took out my phone and checked whether the location I had labelled on Google Maps was saved. I now knew how to find her home. And I planned to return as soon as possible.

The walk to the town was shortened after I hitched a ride in a small truck heading to the market to sell homemade goodies. I bought a few of their products when they refused to let me pay.

When I reached the basecamp hotel, I found my bro-gang having breakfast. Naveen looked up just as I was entering the cafeteria and raised his hand to greet me.

"Look who is here. My errant brother has returned," he said once I reached their table.

"Come and sit. Have breakfast," said Arjun, who was polishing off the last pieces of a *dosa*.

"It's okay. I had breakfast at the place where I stayed," I said. Immediately, Aathira's face popped up in my mind's eye. The corners of my lips lifted as I recalled all that had transpired the previous night. If I told them that I had met the girl of my dreams, how would they react? Knowing them, I knew the news would reach the ladies' gang within minutes and then young and old alike would jump onto the bandwagon to get me married as soon as possible.

"Something is seriously wrong. Was that a smile I saw on your lips now? You had your poker face on throughout the trip. What changed? You don't look like someone who was lost. You look like someone who is back after doing something forbidden," said Vishal, wrinkling his brow.

"Yeah. Looks like he went to visit his secret lover," said Kishore, narrowing his eyes and searching my face.

I grinned. I wasn't ready to tell them about Aathira. Not yet. I wanted her to remain my secret. My beautiful little secret.

"You might have had quite a harrowing ordeal after getting lost. Tell us what happened. Where did you stay?" asked Arjun. Naveen and Vishal had stopped eating and looked eager to hear my reply.

"I found a house in the hills and I stayed the night in their outhouse. In the morning, they helped me get to the main road that led to the town. That's it," I said. I hadn't uttered a single lie. But I had managed to camouflage the truth.

"So boring. I thought I might hear a tiger-chased-me tale. Or at least that a wild pig scared you," said Vishal.

"Nothing as wild as that," I said much to their dismay.

"Why is it that I am finding that hard to believe? Is it just me or do you all feel he is hiding something?" asked Vishal

The others agreed with him that my story had gaping holes.

"You guys...," I said with a chuckle.

"Did you hear that? He laughed. He actually laughed. Our in-house billionaire really laughed," exclaimed Kishore.

"He is obviously hiding something. We will gang up with the others and find a way to get that out of him at Sreepuram," said Naveen.

"Yes. Let's leave after lunch then. I have to shop for some things I promised to take home," said Vishal. "I am missing my darlings already."

The others also expressed similar wishes. I envied that they had found true love. I had finally fallen in love. Yet, my boat of love was still stranded at sea, with no hope of reaching the shore. I missed Aathira like we had been separated after being together for years.

How could I miss her so much? It didn't make sense. I hadn't known about her existence until yesterday evening. But now, she had become the most important person in this whole world to me. I wanted to love her, protect her and have her beside me always. The urge to turn around and go and find her was becoming overwhelming with each second that ticked away.

My mobile pinged with another reminder. It was time for the conference call. Time to turn on my 'I-got-this' mode. Leaving my cousins to finish their breakfast, I returned to the silence of my room to connect with our overseas client.

An hour flew by as we—Rohit and I—discussed the project brief for the app our client wanted us to design. They had many demands and the list of the services the app had to provide was really long. My client ran a holistic health organization and he wanted the app to give their customers access to meditations, both live and recorded. They also required a community space within the app where those who signed up could interact. Online workshops, resources on mental health and also a forum to interact with certified doctors and professionals from various health sciences were also on their list of requirements. They even wanted some interactive games included. It had taken us two weeks of hard work for our team to come up with the project brief.

It seemed like a challenging yet interesting project. The work would keep the team in charge of the project at Quarks Info Solutions busy for the next eight or nine months. The next few weeks would be truly hectic for them. Our developers would research the ideas first, then the design sprints would eat up six to twelve weeks. Development and prototyping could take six to twelve weeks. Deploying it to the app stores would take a few more weeks. We were also bound by contract to provide continuous improvement and post-launch support to them for the next five years.

With twenty recruits joining our team soon, Quarks now had a strength of thousand plus employees. We were accepting more work and diversifying our revenue streams. The success of our apps had made us a name to reckon in the Asian app creation industry and there was a constant in-flow of new clients.

As soon as the client logged off, I slumped into my chair. And immediately, my thoughts wandered back to Aathira. Rohit hadn't logged off and he raised his eyebrows as he looked at me.

"You have that look on your face now," he said.

"What look?"

"As if there is this nagging problem that you need to solve immediately," he explained.

His words reflected how well he knew me. He could read my mind like a pro. This was the reason we had bonded right from the first day of college. I had moved to the college hostel in the final year and our friendship had deepened.

"In fact there is. And it is killing me," I said. Rohit was a good listener and I really needed to vent.

"What is it, bro? Is there anything I can do to help?"

I sighed and then shrugged.

"No one can. Except for the person concerned. And unfortunately, she is in no mood to help," I confessed reluctantly. I watched his eyes widen.

"Aha, she? A girl finally. I am thrilled. Tell me everything. You know I am an expert at solving problems in that area," he said.

Rohit was indeed an expert in the field. He resembled some famous South Korean actor(I forgot what his name was) and had been a heart-breaker right from college. Girls threw themselves at him everywhere and he shamelessly took advantage of it. And yet, he had successfully managed to remain single. None of his relationships lasted for more than a month.

As far as rumours went, he could make any girl fall for him. In college, we used to maintain a ledger and place bets as to whether or not he would win the heart of a girl. He had only success stories when it came to such conquests. But his heart was not involved in any of those affairs. He flitted from girl to girl like a bee on flowers. The moment he felt the girl was becoming a bit clingy, he ended it. I wasn't sure whether I could rely on his relationship advice. But he knew how to win a girl's heart. I had no idea how to convince Aathira to give our relationship a chance.

"This is not your kind of romance. This is my kind and I am a hundred per cent serious," I said.

If there was one topic we couldn't agree upon, it was love. He didn't believe in the forever kind of love. I did. He was interested in only casual relationships. I would never involve myself in a fling.

I understood why Rohit didn't believe in my kind of love. His mother had been a South Korean heiress and his father belonged to a rich aristocratic family in Kerala. They fell in love while his father was working in South Korea. They got married after much opposition from both families. Sadly, his mother died a few days after Rohit's birth. His father was forced to remarry so Rohit could have a mother figure. But he never really loved his new wife and that often caused fights. His dysfunctional family, I believed, was the reason Rohit didn't believe in love or marriage.

"Noted. More details, please," he said as he leaned back in his chair. He pushed back the hair from his forehead only to allow them to fall back like a silk curtain on his forehead. His silky hair was as popular as the rest of him. All the girls loved it and the guys envied it.

I started right at the beginning and told him briefly how I had met Aathira and fallen in love with her. In doing so, I relived the magic of meeting her again in my mind's eye and my heart began a salsa.

When I finished narrating everything, Rohit shook his head with a smile.

"I don't think you did anything wrong. As far as I know, girls prefer perfect gentlemen like you. You acted like one. You want to go back and find her right now, don't you?" he asked.

I nodded. "Before leaving Wayanad, I am planning to drive to her place and talk to her."

"Don't do that. Give it a month's time minimum, and if you still think she is the one for you, go and find her. God, I must see this girl who has managed to sway our sworn bachelor," he said.

His words did make sense. Going back to the hills to search for her would prompt more questions from my cousins and brother too. And her parents would be horrified if they learned of all that had transpired yesterday.

"I have a feeling, you will approve of my choice," I said. Even though I didn't condone his womanizing, he was my closest friend and I valued his opinion.

"I can't wait to meet her," said Rohit.

I couldn't either. I wasn't sure how I would endure a month of not seeing her or not taking a single step to find her. But it had to be done.

10

Aathira

To compensate for a sleepless night and the exertion from the morning, I took a nap after reaching home. When I woke up, everything about the previous night felt like a dream. I lay on the bed and closed my eyes hoping to go back into that sweet dream.

A stranger meeting a heartbroken girl and falling head over heels in love with her.... Such things happened in the books I read. Never in my life. Was it a dream?

Just to make sure that whatever happened wasn't a dream, I went to the outhouse to check for evidence that Navneet had been there. I found my father's track pants and T-shirt folded haphazardly and discarded on the bed. A novel lay on the pillow.

I sat on the bed and exhaled deeply. I tried to recall how he looked. It did not take a whole lot of effort; I remembered him perfectly. His eyes, his lips, and especially his smile were imprinted deeply in my heart. Sleep had diminished the clarity of some of the moments but I remembered several other moments with razor-sharp clarity. But I didn't want to forget anything. So, I forced myself to remember. I forced myself to relive the magic that had happened the night before and earlier that day.

I dearly wished I hadn't insisted that we forget what had happened. What would have happened if we had exchanged numbers? I had numbers of even some of the people I hated on my phone.

What the heck could have happened anyway if we had exchanged email addresses? We were adults. Relationships were born out of fond moments. A smile, a random touch, a prank call…. Many love stories in our college had begun with much less than what we had shared.

College reminded me of the STAR Quartet and I remembered that our campus interview results were to be published today. It was almost twelve. How had I forgotten?

Just as I turned on the broadband WiFi, the landline rang. It was Trisha.

"Girl, where were you? Have you checked your email?" she asked when I answered.

"I was just about to. You got in anywhere?" I asked, suddenly anxious. What if I didn't get in?

"I did. But the other two didn't. You check. I don't want to be all alone, yaar," whined Trisha.

The WiFi connection turned on just then and my phone started to ping with notifications. The top notification was an email from our top recruiter, Quarks Info Solutions.

Was it a rejection or an acceptance? With my heart pounding in my ribs, I clicked on the notification.

Congratulations, Miss Aathira Iyappan.

You have been selected to be a part of our App Development team.

If you wish to accept this job offer,

reply to this email and report at the training office located at …

I jumped up and down with glee. Oh my God, I had made it!

"Trisha, I got selected too. In Quarks," I screamed into the phone.

"Yay. Me too. At least we both will be together," said Trisha.

"Too bad the other two didn't get placed," I said. If Sneha and Riddhi had also got selected, it would have been so awesome.

"Open WhatsApp. Tell the others. I wonder who else from our college got in," said Trisha.

According to the info from our placement cell, there were twenty openings in Quarks Info Solutions. Surely, someone else from our college would have also got in.

Though delighted that I had got into a top company, I knew I would miss our quartet. I had hoped that all four of us would get placed in QIS. We had studied hard and the exam had also gone well. But alas, someone else must have done better.

Once I opened Whatsapp, I was sucked into a discussion about our future at Quarks and also about what the future was looking like for the others. I joined the discussion.

Riddhi: Girls, as I haven't been selected by any of the companies, I might give in to family pressure and grab that offer of doing an MBA in London.

Sneha: Good for you! I wish my family was as rich and magnanimous. They are hounding me with marriage proposals already. Help me, God.

Trisha: I heard Quarks is expanding its operations. Maybe they will go on another recruitment drive soon. You will get in next time, Sneha.

Me: Yeah. But promise me guys, wherever we are, we will remain in touch always. STAR Quartet should never

die.

All of them agreed immediately.

Trisha: Let's switch to video call. We need to make a solemn promise now that our separation is imminent.

I panicked. One look at me and they would know. But I couldn't escape now, could I?

I sighed. I would have to tell them everything. Anyway, if they knew I was keeping this big a secret, they would right away oust me from the WhatsApp group. According to our resolution, there shouldn't be a secret within the STAR Quartet.

Riddhi was in her bathtub enjoying a bubble bath. Sneha and Trisha were in their rooms at their respective homes.

"Oye, Riddhi. I miss that bathtub of yours," Sneha sighed.

We had all visited Riddhi's home in Kochi during the semester break and had a blast. We had taken turns soaking ourselves in warm, fragrant water in her spacious Italian bathtub.

"Come over anytime. I miss you guys. I have no idea how I am going to live in a country where it never stops raining. You know how much I hate rains," said Riddhi.

"Did you forget you always wanted to experience a white Christmas? Now you will be able to. I am so jealous," I said, trying to appear bubbly.

"Can someone get my parents to stop pushing me into an arranged marriage with some stranger? I am panicking here. This afternoon also some idiot is going to come and visit me. I hate these ridiculous blind dates they arrange for me," said Sneha.

"Wait a minute. What happened to you, Aathira? You look like you haven't slept in years. Your eyes look red and you have bags under your eyes. Are you alright?" exclaimed Trisha.

Oops. The full focus of all three was now on me. I sighed realizing that my time was up. Time to come clean.

I raised my hand and said, "I have something to confess. I did go to see Pratik yesterday."

"WHAT?" all three cried in unison.

"You said you went for a wedding."

"I lied," I said.

"Are you saying you confessed to that bastard and he rejected you? Is that why you are looking like the female version of Devdas?" asked Riddhi. She was sitting up in the tub now and had not noticed that her boobs were partially out of the water now.

"No. I didn't confess to him. But I heard him tell Daisy that he'd never make things official with me. 'She has a huge crush on me and would do anything to please me. I've used her wisely, haven't I?' Those were his exact words," I managed to say.

No one spoke for a few seconds and then all three of them started showering curses on Pratik simultaneously.

"Oh, I can't believe someone can be this big a douchebag. He was with Daisy after promising to meet you?" screamed Riddhi. She switched the camera to avoid being seen as she stepped out of the tub. She was back again a few seconds later wrapped in a bathrobe.

Daisy was our junior in college and clung to Pratik like a sloth. She was pretty and belonged to one of the richest families in Wayanad.

"That idiot will have to eat his words very soon. Who will do his dirty works now that you know his true colours?" said Sneha.

"Does he know that you heard them?" asked Trisha.

"No. They were waiting outside the cafe where we were supposed to meet. Daisy was whining as to why he was meeting me and he told her that I was just a convenience."

"Oh, I want to kill him!" cried Sneha. "I wish I could give you a tight hug, dear. As Trisha said, it is good that you realized his devious behaviour before it was too late. It is time you forgot that idiot."

Riddhi and Trisha nodded in agreement

"Would you all believe me if I say that I burned all my journals?" I asked.

"YOU DID?" screamed Riddhi.

"Wow," exclaimed Sneha.

"That's my girl," said Trisha, pumping a fist in the air.

"I did. And I promise that from today onward, I will not speak a word about Pratik," I declared, keeping my right hand on my heart.

"And we are all your witnesses. I have a feeling that you will meet a better guy and have your first kiss at QIS," teased Riddhi.

I blushed as I recalled what else had happened yesterday.

"Look at her. She is blushing as if she has already kissed someone and remembered it when you said that, Riddhi," said Trisha.

These girls! Was it possible to hide anything from them?

"Did you kiss that idiot, Aathira?" asked Sneha, her eyes wide. If I said yes, she might perhaps faint. She hated the guy with a vengeance.

"No. Not Pratik," I said.

"Not Pratik? Then who?" It was Trisha.

"Someone good. Someone who is not Pratik. Someone whom I might not meet ever again," I blurted out the truth.

The silence that followed was terrifying. I glanced at the faces of my best friends and they were gaping at me like they had seen a ghost. They hadn't expected this from me. They would understand if Trisha had spoken these words or even Riddhi. Sneha and I never ventured into anything beyond daydreaming about our crushes.

Trisha was the first to recover.

"Out with all the details. I will personally come and grab your hair now if you leave anything out," she said.

"Yes, I am getting on the next train if you don't talk," said Riddhi.

Sneha also came out with a similar threat and I told them everything that had passed.

"Oh my God, this sounds so filmy... are you sure you haven't conjured up this guy in your dreams?" Sneha sighed.

"Girl, I didn't know you were this brave. You almost had a one-night stand," said Riddhi.

"Shut up. Nothing of that sort occurred," I protested.

"You are an idiot. You shouldn't have asked him to forget all about it. Girl, you might have just kicked your only chance at love goodbye," said Sneha, the forever romantic among us.

Sneha had given words to my fear. What if I never met him again? I didn't think I would ever meet anyone who could compare to Navneet.

"You did the right thing, Aathira. I am impressed. You were clever in not letting him know you were alone. He might not have stopped at a kiss if he had known. That is what happens in all the K-Dramas I watch. A kiss leads right to the bedroom," said Trisha, the K-drama addict.

"As if!" I protested. I was sure nothing of that sort would have happened. Navneet didn't seem like such a person. He would have kept things sane.

"I still think you shouldn't have rejected him. He arrived at your doorstep on the day your heart broke... That's definitely a sign," said Sneha.

"What sign?! Anyway, thank the guy for helping you forget that bastard. I permit you to keep on blushing by thinking about your dog-whisperer," said Riddhi.

"Yeah, he seems okay enough to tease you constantly with," said Trisha.

And just like that, they began to ship me with a stranger. I knew I would continue to hear about my dog-whisperer like he was my other half. Every day, every hour from now on!

11

Navneet

Sreepuram, July 31, 2019

The blissful month with the Sreepuram family was going exactly according to plan until my enchanting girl from the hills stormed into my life.

With my thoughts running in loops around Aathira, it became a struggle to pay attention to the conversations and activities happening around me.

My cousins left me alone for a week, which in itself was a miracle. Then on a Sunday, while we were relaxing after our evening tea, they launched a joint attack on me.

I was sitting and sulking on a corner chair on the back verandah wondering if I would meet Aathira ever again.

"Is something wrong with the company, Navneet?" asked Arjun, and immediately, the chatter around me ceased.

"No. Why do you ask?" I said wondering what had prompted him to ask that.

"Really? You have been so absent-minded these past few days. We need to ask twice to get an answer from you. Something is certainly amiss," said Kishore.

"Yeah. Tell us. Can we help in any way?" asked Ananya.

"I am perfectly okay. Nothing is wrong," I lied.

"Don't lie. You have been not yourself ever since we returned from Wayanad. What happened?" asked Naveen.

"Even I felt so. Something definitely happened there," said Kishore.

"Leave him alone, guys. We all have mood swings, don't we?" said Arya, much to the surprise of others.

I grinned at her but cringed internally. That statement just meant she was going to grill me later. She exchanged glances with Naveen that clearly said they'd have to deal with this privately. I knew I had to step up and mitigate whatever damage my moodiness had inflicted on the group.

"Okay, relax. There were some app design issues that we were struggling with. But it's going to be sorted out soon. So, relax," I said, partially telling the truth.

One of our new clients had more demands which meant added complexity in the design. But it was not a thing that couldn't be handled.

That let me off the hook for the time being and I tried my maximum to join in their banter. But every second, the face of my girl from the hills popped up in my mind's eye and derailed my focus. I didn't think I would last for even another week without being able to contact her or see her, let alone a month.

That night, I tried to find Aathira online. When I began my sleuthing, I realized I hardly knew anything about her other than her first name. Still, I looked her up on all social media platforms I had signed up on and on popular forums that were frequented by engineering students. My mission was a failure mainly because too many results came up when I searched her name.

Since I'd not checked social media for almost a year, my inbox was flooded with messages from old acquaintances and friends. Now that I had become successful and a name to be reckoned with in the IT world, more and more people were reaching out to me seeking jobs, recommendations and whatnot.

I ignored most of them but responded to some messages from a few old friends. Then I plunged myself back into searching for Aathira.

Within an hour of fruitless snooping around online, I decided I wasn't going to postpone my Wayanad trip. I had to find her. Else, the longing in my heart was going to make my heart conk out.

When we gathered again after dinner, my cousins, aunts and Ammamma decided to focus on me again. This time my mistake was that I was the last eligible bachelor in the family.

"Ammamma is worried that you will remain a bachelor," said my mother beginning what was to become a combined attack from all those gathered.

"People, please leave me alone. I don't even get time to breathe with all the added responsibilities I have. I cannot think of marriage for another five years," I said.

"Five years? You will be quite old by then," protested Ammamma.

"I am just thirty now. I will be as old as Naveen is now in another five years. Should I remind you all that Naveen got married just last year?" I asked, determined to ward off any potential blind dates that I'd be forced to go to. My Ammamma and aunts were experts at arranging marriages in my family.

I didn't think arranged marriages were bad. After all, my parents and several others in the family had had their marriages arranged and none of them was on the verge of a divorce.

But I didn't want an arranged marriage. I wanted a love marriage. The kind my brother had. The kind my cousins had.

My cousin Kishore was the oldest among us, but the kind of love that existed between Shreya and him was one that I wished to have for myself one day. Strong, steady and ever-evolving.

Ananya and Arjun set relationship goals with the way they helped each other grow.

Vishal and Shalini made me want to believe that love could overcome anything.

My brother and Arya's story was a different one entirely. Even after being separated for years, the way they had found each other and rekindled their love made my heart fill with happiness and hope.

"Do you think I would have waited if I'd found Arya earlier?" asked Naveen.

"What I meant is, it's okay to wait," I said.

"Who knows how long I will be alive. I do wish to see your wife before I leave this earth," said Ammamma.

Absolute silence filled the living room where we were all seated. Ammamma was not someone who tried to blackmail by flashing her death card. This was new.

"What Amma? Don't say such things. You are certainly going to outlive us," said my mother.

"Come on, Ammamma. Don't scare us by saying such things. Besides, who here is as health-conscious and disciplined as you?" asked Ananya.

Ammamma was dear to every one of us. Even the thought of her being gone felt like a terrible shock.

"Okay, okay, now don't be upset over that. I was just stating a fact. Navneet, tell me what type of a girl would you want as your wife?" asked Ammamma.

I decided to lighten the mood and indulge her. I closed my eyes and thought of Aathira. Then I described her to everyone.

"My dream girl is someone who will take my breath away at first sight. Curly, jasmine-scented hair that reaches her hips, doe eyes that sparkle brightly, pearly white teeth, bud-like lips. Maybe about five feet seven inches tall, with skin that is soft like rose petals and yes, with a body like that of Aphrodite. And she should be an engineer as well," I declared with a grin.

Silence danced like a tornado in the room for a long minute.

Vishal was the first to react.

"That certainly wasn't a fantasy. You were clearly describing someone you met," he screamed.

"Exactly," said Arjun.

I chuckled. Now their imaginations would run wild.

"You asked for it and I gave you a very vivid picture. That is all," I said.

"Um. If you say so. Radha, do you know anyone that fits that description?" Ammamma asked my mother.

"I don't think so. Is there anyone in our acquaintance who looks like that?" my mother wondered aloud.

Now that I had given enough fodder for their brains to go into overdrive, I leaned back into my chair and enjoyed their banter fully directed at me.

The Sreepuram family was unique. There was no one like us. I could easily imagine Aathira seated among them. Being pampered by them and being the centre of their attention.

Where are you, dear? Will you remain elusive forever?

12
Aathira

July 31, 2019, Kannur

The Baader-Meinhof phenomenon or the frequency illusion is defined as a cognitive bias where something you recently learned about or noticed seemed to appear everywhere. I had come across this concept while surfing the internet randomly the other day.

Now I was experiencing it first hand.

In my case, the name Navneet popped up everywhere, when I least expected it. Like, the other day, Appa brought home a tea cake from a bakery in town called Navneet bakery. I hadn't ever heard of that bakery. Never.

The private bus I took today morning to my mother's ancestral home was owned by Navneet Travels. What a coincidence!

Not only me, but the bug seemed to have affected my girls' gang as well. The STAR Quartet messaged me whenever and from wherever they came across his name. I had starred all the messages where he had been the topic of discussion so that I could scroll through them whenever I needed. Crazy, I know!

I opened my starred messages section and started reading them for the second time this morning. Because, why not!

Riddhi: Apparently, 'Navneet' means fresh butter. Considering how utterly-butterly he won over your heart, that name suits him. It's also one of the names of the mischievous lil Krishna. *eye roll emoji* Explains everything!

Sneha: Yikes. The name Navneet is everywhere. The guy who is coming to see me this evening is called Navneet. *three laughing emojis*

Trisha: Lol. I am dying here. He seems determined to haunt you, Aathira. *ghost emoji*

His name seemed to jump into my awareness at least once every hour without fail. Maybe it was because my thoughts were fixated on that one person and that one magical night that I'd remember for the rest of my life. I didn't expect anything else to follow. Or that was what I told my friends. But within the depths of my heart, I hid an ardent wish to meet him again. I wished I could go back to that night once more, relive it and make a different decision in the end.

With a sigh, I continued browsing through more recent messages.

Sneha: My Navneet turned out to be a fat fellow with a beer belly. I wonder how my parents even considered him for me! I am not even a quarter his size.

Riddhi: Lol. Then your Navneet might crush your ribs on your first night if you get married to him.

Sneha: Shut up. As if I would marry that nerd.

Just when I was about to close WhatsApp, Riddhi pinged.

Riddhi: Guys, breaking news. I got in at IIM Bangalore. I didn't think I would be able to but finally, I am in! * three dancing girl emojis* Waiting list rocks.

Me: Girl, that is amazing! Congratulations.

Trisha: Yay! That means you will be in Bangalore as well.

Riddhi: Yes. Let's live together. My father is already searching for ready-to-move-in flats in the area.

Sneha: Congratulations, babe. But I am so sad!! *three teary-faced emojis* You guys will be together. I will be the only one left out. *three more teary-faced emojis*

Trisha: Sneha dear, we will find a way to be together soon.

Riddhi: Girls, that means I need to make a quick trip to the college to get my transfer certificate. Is anyone joining me?

Me: I will come.

Trisha: Me too.

Sneha: I am in as well. Let's make this last trip to college absolutely special.

Trisha: Aathira, darling, will you be able to? I heard you guys are in the process of moving to your new place, right?

Me: Yes. I have finished packing all my stuff. Appa's friends are going to help him move the stuff. I moved to Amma's place in Kannur. I will only be going to our new place once the shifting is complete. They want me to just focus on moving to Bangalore.

Appa had decided to shift as soon as possible. Today was his last working day at the estate. And once the send-off party was over, our last connection with the estate would be officially terminated. I had thought my father would be distraught after retiring. But it seems like my parents had come up with a plan already.

My parents bonded the best in the kitchen. They cooked together every day. I don't remember a time when Appa hadn't helped Amma in the kitchen. When they had returned from the reception that day, they were brimming with newfound energy. They had formulated the perfect retirement plan. They were going to open a tiny restaurant on the outskirts of the town to indulge in what they loved the most—cooking.

A traditional house cum restaurant on the outskirts of the town had closed business and the owners were moving to a different state. They were looking for new tenants. Someone had mentioned it to Appa at the reception and he had wholeheartedly dived into the new plan. Appa had transformed from a brooding retiree to an aspiring restaurateur within a day. Every day from then on, my parents spent hours together planning the menu they wanted to put up and other details.

I was happy that whatever I had dreaded wasn't going to happen. My Appa was not going to brood and moan after he retired.

We visited our new home the very next day. The building was smaller compared to the bungalow we had been living in but it was a three BHK home with a restaurant set up on the ground floor. So, they had gone for it. We were to live above our restaurant.

It was hard for me to leave the place that had been our home for the last five years. So many fond memories had been added recently as well. Memories of my first kiss, my first heartbreak and that one magical night with my dog whisperer. But, sometimes, moving on was the best remedy. When the time was ripe, we had to let go of the old to make space for the new.

The new assistant manager was to move in with his family in the third week of August. In another three weeks, that house would become someone else's home. Someone else would sleep in the room where I used to sleep.

It was slightly distressing. But is there anything constant in life other than change? I was anyway shifting to Bangalore in mid-August as our training was beginning on August 19th.

A message notification ended my reverie.

Riddhi: Awesome. Can't wait to roam the campus with you girls tomorrow.

Trisha: Yay! Let's meet at around eleven near the gate. We will have lunch at the Friendzz one more time once we get the TC.

Me: Yesss! I am craving their fruit salad right now.

Trisha: My mouth is watering just thinking about theirPazham pori.

Sneha: Pazham pori! Don't say that name again. I am drowning in my drool here.

Riddhi: I am craving their Prawns Biriyani. Drool!! Let me rush and book my plane ticket to Kannur.

With our plans thus made, we all set about getting ready to meet again at our alma mater.

August 1, 2019, Kannur

Being back on campus brought back so many good memories of the fun I had with my girls' gang. The campus was greener after the rain and the blooming flowers heralded the onset of spring. This was my favourite time of the year on campus.

We roamed around once we cleared all our dues and got our transfer certificates. The TCs in our hands officially ended our connection to our college. Four years of bliss and learning had finally come to an end. We decided to visit our teachers before we left.

As we were the nerds of our class, we were received enthusiastically by our lecturers. Most of them wanted to know whether we were going for higher studies or joining jobs. After chatting with them for a few minutes, we left the campus.

We were on our way out when a white BMW slowed down next to the campus gate and a pretty woman got out.

"Arya Ma'am!" screamed Sneha. We all rushed toward our former teacher who had been our project guide in the seventh semester. She'd been such an inspiration to us. She was married to a celebrity YouTuber and astrologer, who was also an alumnus of our college.

"Hey! It's such a pleasure to meet you girls again. How are you all doing?" said Arya Ma'am, greeting us warmly.

"We are all doing fine, Ma'am. How are you? Will you be resuming work at the college this semester?" asked Riddhi.

"No, I won't, girls. I have moved to Bangalore and joined my husband's firm," said Arya ma'am.

"Oh, Bangalore? Three of us are going to be there in Bangalore too. Riddhi has enrolled for her MBA at IIM, Bangalore. And Aathira and I are starting jobs at an MNC there," said Trisha.

"That's awesome. How about you, Sneha? What are your plans?" asked Arya Ma'am.

"Most likely I will be married by the end of the year, given the pace at which my parents are looking at proposals. They are not even letting me work for some time. They want me out of the way. After all, I am the eldest among their three daughters," whined Sneha.

"Oh ho. That's sad. Perhaps you should try and convince them that a girl with a job has better chances in the marriage market than a jobless graduate," said Arya Ma'am with a wink.

We all chuckled. We had never seen this side of Arya Ma'am. When she was our lecturer, she used to be a good teacher but was gloomy and lost in her thoughts. Now she seemed like a different person altogether. Happiness radiated from her.

"Why didn't I think of that? Maybe I still can escape from the marriage train somehow," said Sneha.

"But I should tell you. Marriages are not all that bad, you know. If it is with the right person, it can be super fun," she said.

She looked at her husband who was getting out of the car and waved at him. Trisha, who was a big fan of Arya Ma'am's husband Naveen, sucked in the air and went all mute when he joined us. Arya Ma'am and her husband made a fine pair. We had all become his fans when he had given a talk on Vedic astrology at the campus last year. He looked even more handsome and happier than he had appeared back then. Marriage suited him clearly. He greeted us and then turned to his wife.

"I will come with you to see your friend. I would rather spend time walking with you around the compound than hear his snores," said Naveen, pointing at the car.

"Navneet is still asleep? Didn't he say he wanted to look around the campus as well?" asked Arya Ma'am.

At the mention of the name Navneet, my gang suddenly snapped to full attention. Trisha even started elbowing me continuously. Ugh, were they going to tease me every time some guy named Navneet crossed our path?

"He might be doing that right now in his dreams. He kicked me when I tried to wake him up," said Naveen.

Arya Ma'am chuckled. "Let him sleep peacefully then. The poor guy was probably working late last night," said Arya.

"Yeah. Let's go," said Naveen.

The couple bid us goodbye and walked toward the main block. The moment they left, the trio surrounded me.

"Should we check on *the* Navneet in the car? What if it is *your* Navneet?" asked Riddhi and she took a step toward the car.

My heart thundered for no reason. I tried to dissuade the trio but they went and circled the car once before proceeding toward Friendzz, giggling loudly.

After glancing furtively at the car just once when I was right in front of the car, I ran and joined them. In my hurry, I hadn't seen anything of use.

"Look at her face! She has gone all red. Anyway, that is not the Navneet who came to see me. This guy looked taller," said Sneha when I caught up with them.

"Was he awake?" I asked, tentatively.

"I don't think he was. He had a baseball cap pulled low on his face and was sleeping like a baby," said Riddhi. "He might not be bad looking given whose brother he is. Maybe we should have created some ruckus and woken him up."

"You girls are crazy," I said. Given how lucky I was, there was hardly any chance that he was the same Navneet.

But what if it was? Was I ready to face him again?

"Of course not! We are just curious. We are looking out for you, babe," said Trisha.

I rolled my eyes. "Come, let's go in. Otherwise, we won't find a free table," I said and dragged the trio into the restaurant.

We found a table and I took the seat that faced the window. I kept my eyes trained on the car hoping that the Navneet in the car might open the door and step out to stretch his limbs. But nothing of that sort happened for the next half an hour. Arya Ma'am and her husband returned before we finished lunch. The car moved away from the college gate, mingled with the traffic on the main road and disappeared from my view within seconds.

Somehow, one question kept nagging me again and again. What if it had indeed been my dog-whisperer inside the car? Had I kicked away another chance of meeting him? A chance that destiny had thrown my way?

I didn't know. But strangely, the thought that it had been my Navneet continued to raise its head every now and then.

My Navneet?

I shrugged to make the crazy thought go away. As usual, like a stuck key on the keyboard, it continued to haunt me.

13

Navneet

August 1, 2019, Kannur

I'd thought I was dreaming.

Hearing giggles, I opened my eyes. Aathira appeared right in front of my car dressed in a red churidar—beautiful like a Goddess— gaped at me and then ran away. Disturbed by how my dreams always ended in this manner, with her running away from me, I sank back into the seat and went back to sleep.

Hours later, Naveen's booming laughter woke me up.

"Can't you guys keep it down a bit? Mind sharing what it was that made you laugh?" I asked, bored.

"Oh, so you have finally woken up. Didn't you say you wanted to visit the campus once again?" asked Arya.

"I did. But obviously, you didn't wake me up. We are almost at Sreepuram already," I said.

"Not because we didn't try. I poked you so much but you wouldn't wake up. We had a pleasant walk around the campus," said Naveen. Given how he was looking at Arya with bedroom eyes they might have even made use of one of those make-out spots inside the campus. He still couldn't keep his hands to himself when she was around him.

"What is the use of crying over spilt milk anyway. I will visit it on our way back," I said, trying to not think about my brother making out with my best friend.

"Oh, and we met someone who could pass off as your dream girl. Checked all your boxes. Curly hair that reaches the hips, doe-like eyes, and of course, she is an engineer," said Naveen with a mischievous grin.

There he went again. After I had spoken of my dream girl, these guys seemed to see her everywhere. Of course, none of the girls they pointed out to me was Aathira.

"Aathira would have made a good co-sister though. Very bright and beautiful. She was a member of the Star Quartet, my favourite bunch of students in college," said Arya.

My breath whooshed out of me when I heard her mention Aathira and her gang. What in the world had I missed?

"What did you just say?" I asked, unable to comprehend that what I had thought to be a dream might not have been one.

"Oh did me mentioning some girl as my co-sister offend you?"

"No, the gang's name. Sounds interesting. Why are they called so?" I asked, trying to confirm that she had been indeed talking about Aathira's gang.

"They call themselves the STAR Quartet. They are four best friends. The name of the group is coined from the first letter of their names. S for Sneha, T for Trisha, A for Aathira and R for Riddhi. Genius, right? They were true stars on the campus. Almost everyone knew them. They were good at studies and extracurricular activities alike. That is why I loved them. Aathira is a trained classical dancer, and Sneha plays the violin beautifully. Trisha sings, and Riddhi is a star badminton player. I was the adviser for their project before I quit and hence got to know them well," Arya explained.

Aathira was a trained classical dancer? No wonder her dance moves were so perfect.

"Nice," I said, but mentally cursed myself for falling asleep. That too I had gone back to sleep after being woken up by her presence.

Naveen then talked about one of his lecturers they had just met and shared a funny story from his time on campus.

I zoned out thinking about my girl. Perhaps this was a sign. Destiny was throwing her into my path again and I wanted to believe that this wouldn't be the last. I wouldn't allow it to be the last time she and I met. Perhaps Arya had her number. She'd share it with me if I asked. After all, she was still my best friend and she liked Aathira. I was relieved that now, I had a solid way to connect with Aathira.

Anyway, I was going to visit her place the next weekend and try to convince Aathira that we were meant to be together. Until then, I wasn't going to ask Arya for her number.

My eyes fell on the red-light blinking on the car dash cam and my heart did a happy jig. I had a way to verify if it was indeed Aathira! I had the urge to pull out the memory card from the dash cam then and there but I decided to wait.

"I want to go out for a bit. Leave the key in here," I said as Naveen parked the car in the courtyard of Sree Nilayam. I rushed to my room to grab my laptop and earpods and was back in the car within fifteen minutes. I drove to a football ground nearby.

Once there, I took out the memory card of the dash cam and inserted it into my laptop and waited with bated breath for it to load. Rewinding to the time we must have been in front of the campus, I found what I was looking for. My heart raced as if it was the main competitor in a Formula One event.

There she was. She was dressed in a red churidar and her hair was cascading over her shoulders like a monsoon cloud. Her face was visible only for a fraction of a minute. The way she furtively glanced at the car made me wonder if she knew I was in there.

Had Arya or Naveen mentioned my name to her? Had she seen my face? Was that why she was running away? My heart sank at the thought.

I rewound it and watched it again. Then, using a software editing tool, I copied that portion of the video onto my laptop into the folder named Aathira. Until now, I had only the photo I had stealthily clicked on the night we met.

Now that I knew where she had studied, which happened to be my college as well, I logged onto Facebook intending to find her online. I looked for her on our college's Facebook page. Hadn't Arya said she was a talented dancer? Chances were that something would turn up.

Facebook didn't disappoint me this time. I found her in the first attempt itself. There were multiple photos of her dancing at various college functions. The one that grabbed my attention was that of her at the inter-collegiate dance festival where she seemed to be the main dancer in a group. Dressed in a cobalt blue, flowing outfit she stood shining like a virtuoso. Her dazzling beauty snatched my breath yet again.

I saved her photos into the same folder on my laptop and clicked the link to her profile. She didn't seem to be a regular on Facebook or her posts were only visible to her friends. Her last public post was about the Kerala floods helpline numbers. I stopped myself from sending her a friend request with humongous effort and quickly closed her profile. I didn't want to come across as a stalker even though I was perhaps the worst sort. I was ogling at her photos like a voyeur.

I wanted to remain that mysterious stranger she met one night for a while longer.

She didn't know who I was, but now I knew so much more about her than before. Again, I took it as a sign that fate was planning to bring us together. I was liking the pace at which the universe was opening up to us. I was loving all the information that was coming my way. She seemed to be just my type. From the Facebook pages she liked, our interests seemed pretty similar. My heart hadn't hummed without any reason.

That evening, I didn't see love arriving. Perhaps Cupid had used his fastest arrow on me. Aathira had already bewitched me before I could even blink. She had crawled deep under my skin and made me question everything I believed about love in one single night.

I was drawn towards her like a moth towards a candle. My sleep had gone for a toss ever since I met her. If this wasn't love, I didn't know what was.

Now the question was, did she love me the way I did?

As for me, she was a beacon in the darkness capable of guiding me towards contentment. Till now, I only had a work life. There was never anyone I cared about other than my immediate family members and friends. Now, she had taken over my grey cells and heartbeats. Work now seemed a bit intimidating because I craved my me-time where I could just lose myself in her thoughts.

All I wanted was to be left alone with her memories. And some nights, I craved to embrace her, trace her lips with mine and make sweet love to her all night till my body was weary and my soul, content.

I reclined in the car seat and relived the memories I had collected and daydreamed about things I wanted to do with her. The places I wanted to visit, the conversations I wanted to have and the gifts I wanted to shower her with. When the longing to hold her in my arms began to bother me again, I revved the car engine back to life and rushed back to Sreepuram.

To dull my senses with family love and to be merry till I could.

ϷϷϷ

August 10, 2019, Wayanad

"Your destination is to your left," announced my GPS and my heart thudded loudly against my ribs.

My heart raced as I plodded through the path I had memorized the last time I walked on it. I sighed in relief when I spotted the giant banyan tree in the path, the small pile of discarded boulders, the wildflower bushes and many more memory markers. I was glad I remembered them all.

I felt like a cad of the worst sort. But I was convinced I had to do this and not leave everything to fate. What the heart wants it just wants. Could anyone in the world fight it?

This was the only way to make my sleepless nights end. This was the only way to make it stop. I wanted to declare to the world that she was mine. But before that, there was a good chance that I'd have to fall on her feet and beg her to give us a chance, to accept me as her lover.

I smiled wildly when I finally spotted her house. I stood there for a few minutes and allowed myself to hope. To hope that Aathira would be there, alone if Lady Luck was on my side and that she too would be eager to meet me again.

With confident steps, I walked into the now-familiar courtyard of the house and looked around. Something seemed off. For one, the courtyard was filled with dry leaves as if it hadn't been swept in days. The flower pots in the verandah had vanished. When I walked closer, I was puzzled to see that the curtains on the windows were also gone. I couldn't see any furniture inside the rooms either. The house looked deserted.

My heart squeezed when I realized that I had lost my chance yet again.

With a heavy heart, I stepped down from the verandah.

Had they left the place?

Just then, a man entered the compound pushing a small push-cart loaded with stuff. He seemed taken aback when he saw me.

"Who are you?" he asked, wrinkling his brow.

"Hi, I came to see my friend who used to live here. Do you know where they are?" I asked, hoping that he might know something.

"I don't know. I am a hired help from the town. I heard the man who lived here retired and left town with his family. I am in charge of re-painting the house before the new family moves in," he said gesturing at the paint buckets on the cart.

Left town? My heart sank.

Thanking him, I plodded to the car and lay my head on the steering wheel, thinking frantically. The only path to Aathira now seemed through Arya. I knew both Arya and my dear brother were going to give me a hard time because I had kept Aathira a secret, but I needed her help. Desperately.

With my decision made, I got back on the road and stopped briefly at 'Iyappan's Family Restaurant', a small roadside restaurant on the outskirts of the town. I didn't remember seeing it last time. Maybe they had opened recently. It seemed like it was run by a husband-wife. The woman sat at the cash counter while the man was taking orders from the customers. The man smiled at me as he served me hot tea that tasted surprisingly great and revived my mood a bit.

"What brings you to Wayanad, young man," he asked, making small talk.

"Just meeting a friend," I said curtly. The man seemed friendly but I was in no mood to talk.

Apart from me, there were only two other customers. I drank the tea, paid the money at the cash counter and left the cafe after politely refusing the man's offer to try the snacks they had on the menu. I didn't think I could handle food; I was afraid I'd puke if I even saw food. I felt dizzy with the speed at which my thoughts were attacking me.

When I reached my car, I heard the sound of a dog barking from somewhere near and I was immediately reminded of Sheru's cute face. I looked around, hoping to spot the source of the sound. It was perhaps coming from the first floor of the building, from inside the house above the restaurant. Maybe it was the hotel owner's dog.

Taking a deep breath, I donned my goggles, and opened the car door, preparing to drive away from the place with a heart heavy with despair.

14
Aathira

August 10, 2019, Wayanad

Sheru's excited barks made me sit up on the bed. He was barking loudly and running around in circles inside the room, before stopping and gazing at something outside the window. What was he excited about? Another rabbit? Or was it a crow?

I kept the novel I was reading on the bed and went to check what Sheru's ruckus was about.

When I looked out of the window, the visual made me freeze and I forgot to breathe. *Navneet?* Was I seeing things? What was he doing here?

I gaped at Navneet as he donned his goggles and got into his car. Even as I desperately wished that he would look up and see me, his car slowly moved onto the road and sped away, vanishing from my sight within seconds.

Sheru whined and moved away from the window. He looked disappointed. His friend hadn't stopped to pamper him. He lay down, resting his head on his front paws and gave me a sidelong glare as if saying that it had been all my mistake.

It had been my doing indeed. I was the one who suggested that I'd keep Sheru in my room as customers at the restaurant might not take kindly to his presence. Especially as he stared at people shamelessly when they were eating and demanded to be fed as if we made him starve.

It seemed like Navneet had stopped at Appa's restaurant. If Sheru had been down there, Navneet would have recognized him immediately. Why did I bring him up?

"I know. I should have let you stay in the restaurant as you wanted. But, my dear, not everyone likes dogs, you know!" I tried to pacify him. He looked away with a sharp bark and closed his eyes. Sheru was mad at me.

Nothing unexpected, my dear Sheru. I was mad at myself.

If I hadn't been obsessed with finishing *Gone with the wind*, the novel I was currently reading before I left for Bangalore, I would have been down there at the restaurant too. Usually, I helped with cleaning and cutting veggies as Amma and Appa prepared lunch. Lunchtime was when we had the maximum number of customers.

Appa had opened the restaurant just five days ago. But already, our restaurant was quite popular among the locals. Even travellers stopped by because it was the last decent one for miles once they left or entered the town. Appa was thrilled that his decision to start this restaurant had been the right one. He missed the estate, but cooking and feeding people, he realized, gave him even more joy than taking care of the estate. And money-wise too, he was doing good.

I looked out of the window once more and sighed. My mobile buzzed with a WhatsApp notification.

It was Sneha, ranting about yet another guy who was going to officially check her out today. Gosh, her parents were relentless. My parents, luckily, hadn't boarded the marriage bandwagon yet. Perhaps once my career took off, they would too. Parents could be a pain in the neck once they started seeking a spouse for their son or daughter. I just hoped the restaurant business would keep my parents occupied and distracted enough to not care about my marital status for a long while.

Me: I want a shoulder to cry on too. *two crying emojis* My Dog-whisperer came to Appa's restaurant just now and I saw him only when he was driving away.

Sneha: What?! You should have run behind his car in filmy style and called out his name. His name would have echoed in the valleys and reached his ears.

Me: Stop it, Sneha! I am so mad that I couldn't go and meet him. I was up here in my room and he was at the restaurant, in the parking, rather. Sheru recognized him and was barking his head off. But Navneet didn't look up. *sad face emoji*

Sneha: *three sad-faced emojis*

Trisha: Jinjja? Daebak!

Me: *eye roll emoji* Now, what does that mean, Trisha?

Trisha was now learning to read and write Korean, which meant we were forced to hear and read Korean daily. Our WhatsApp group had become her practice ground.

Trisha: You guys are such buzz killers. Jinjja? = really? And Daebak! means Oh my God! How are you going to understand my Korean Oppa when you finally meet him?

Riddhi: Stop it, Trisha. I might puke if I hear another Korean word.

Trisha: *five angry face emojis*

Riddhi: We will be good to your Oppa if you stop torturing us daily, okay? Let's focus on the important thing now. Hugs, Aathira. That was sheer bad luck.

Trisha: Maybe he came to search for you.

Me: Could it be? If he had asked around the estate he would have known about Appa's restaurant, right?

Sneha: Yeah. Maybe he came for some other reason. But still, God has thrown him in your path yet another time. Isn't this your second time seeing him?

Me: I think so.

Riddhi: Did you note his car registration number or anything like that? I have a relative working in the traffic department. Maybe we can find his address.

Me: I don't remember anything except that it was a white BMW with a Karnataka registration number. Oh yeah, it had a tricolour sticker on the rear bumper. Light blue, dark blue and red, I think.

Trisha: Girl, you are saved. That looks like the same car Arya ma'am came in. Do you know what that means? The Navneet Arya ma'am was talking about must have been your guy. And you have missed your guy two times in a row now. I clearly remember her car was a BMW and had a Karnataka registration number. It had its brand sticker on the rear bumper.I had noticed it when we had circled the car that day.

My heart was doing something crazy within my rib cage. My fingers trembled as I typed.

Me: Daebak!! Jinjja?

Trisha: Jinjja! And your guy looked hot even though we didn't see his face properly. All muscles at the right places.

Riddhi: Daebak indeed! Girls, shouldn't we plan and find this guy quickly for our sweetum? Karnataka registration number means he might be living in

Bangalore. We have to make you guys meet again. Who knows, you might end up with this guy even before our poor Sneha finds a good one.

Me: I remember he said he worked in Bangalore. Arya Ma'am also lives there, right?

Sneha: Oh, this seems straight out of a romance movie. I really think he came to Wayanad in search of you.

Trisha: Aathira, darling, do you have Arya Ma'am's phone number? You need to contact her.

Me: I don't. And even if I had, how can I call her without a reason?

Riddhi: You are such an idiot. You have plenty of reasons already. She has been living in Bangalore for a long time. You can call her and ask her to recommend a good Mallu restaurant.

Me: That sounds so lame. Google can do that. But anyway, I don't have her number.

Sneha: I have Leena Ma'am's number. She is her best friend, remember?

Riddhi: Ask her. Say we forgot to get her number when we met her the other day.

Sneha: Messaging her right now. She doesn't check her messages that often. If she doesn't respond within a day, I will call her and ask.

Trisha: That's our girl!

They continued to chat but I zoned out. Wow! I couldn't believe that God had put me in his path thrice already within a month. Did he plan something for us? I wish!

My cheeks burned when I remembered our kiss. Navneet had wanted to continue our relationship. But I had gone ahead and poured water on the fire burning bright between us. And now, I desperately wanted to meet him again.

The continuous notifications on my phone demanded my attention. They had stopped talking about Navneet and were now discussing our living arrangements in Bangalore. They must have sensed that I wasn't reading their texts, so they were now switching to a video call.

Riddhi was in her garden, Sneha in her bedroom and Trisha was going somewhere in an auto-rickshaw.

"Girls, my father has found a fully furnished three-bedroom flat in South Bangalore and we can move in immediately. It is near my college and close to your workplace as well. I checked before he signed the documents," said Ridhi.

"Gosh, are you going to be our landlord? I wonder what all you would put us through!" said Trisha.

"Oh, have no doubt! I am going to be a strict house owner. No boys allowed in the apartment, no late-night parties and of course no-one utters a word in Korean there!" teased Riddhi.

Trisha groaned and rolled her eyes.

We had only agreed to be her flatmates if she agreed to accept rent. Riddhi had refused to accept our offer initially but had finally agreed to take a token rent from us.

"I am so jealous of you guys. I just want to die," moaned Sneha.

"When will you stand up to your parents and tell them you don't want to get married now?" asked Riddhi.

"You know I can't. They want me out of the way," said Sneha.

"You can secure a job and move out of the way, my dear. How many times should we tell you? What if the guy you marry wants you to stay at home and look after the kids you both would be making? Would you waste your engineering degree just like that?" asked Riddhi.

"Don't scare me. I am giving in to their demands because they have sacrificed a lot for me," said Sneha.

"So what? You shouldn't be their sacrificial lamb. You should be able to decide your future. Not them. Wouldn't they like it, if you got a good job and earned well? Why else did they pay for your education? Why else did you score so high in your exams? I am sure you can get into a good software firm in Bangalore if you tried. Then we can all be together," said Trisha.

Sneha looked pale. I pitied her. I knew how much she loved her parents and her siblings. She'd been saying right from the beginning of our course that her parents were worried that once she graduated, it would be tougher to get a good groom who didn't demand a huge dowry. Now all the men who sought an alliance with her were either less qualified than her or demanded obscene dowries. Sneha had told her parents clearly that she was against dowry but her parents were not averse to the idea. She wanted to work, but now all her parents wanted was to find her a groom as soon as possible.

"Sneha, sweetheart, don't look so glum. I am sure your parents will find a guy who will support your career dreams. Who knows, he might be just the person you have been waiting for all along," I said, trying to cheer her up.

It was bad enough that she didn't get a job through campus selection. I don't know what I would have done if I had been in her place. I might have perhaps run away from home.

"Will you guys let me crash at your place someday?" asked Sneha.

"Of course, sweetheart. Speak to your parents, put off your marriage plans and come to us. We will help you hunt for a job. Tell them all the good Mallu techies work in

Bangalore. I've heard half of our seniors are right here. Including that guy you used to have a crush on," said Riddhi.

"Don't speak to me of him. He rejected me outright saying I was not his type," said Sneha.

"Not his type, huh? Oh yeah. He likes girls with huge boobies. His last girlfriend was a 40-B. You are no match with your 32-C, my dear," said Trisha.

"Shut up, I am 34-B," protested Sneha.

"My bad! But you are too beautiful to be wasted on a guy like that sweetheart," said Trisha.

"Exactly," said Sneha and tossed her long, pleated hair over her shoulders.

We all laughed together.

"Sneha, don't forget to text Leena Ma'am and ask for Arya Ma'am's number, okay?" I reminded her as we were about to end the call and the others immediately chorused *'ohhhhhhh'!*

I rolled my eyes at their overreaction, while desperately hoping that Navneet was indeed Arya Ma'am's brother-in-law.

15

Navneet

❦

Was the universe telling me to give up? Why else did this happen? I was a hundred per cent sure that I would see Aathira today and convince her that my love for her was sincere. And that, we would begin a lifelong relationship with the blessings of her family.

Was this God's way of telling me that I had to let Aathira go?

The twenty-plus laps I had swum in the village pond had exhausted my energy but my mind was nowhere close to calming down. Floating on my back, I breathed deep, relaxed my body and stared at the stars that were now beginning to shine down upon me.

It was nearing eight in the evening and I hadn't been able to talk to Arya yet about Aathira. My brother had vanished with his wife to God only knew after lunch according to Vishal. I couldn't wait to get Aathira's number from her.

"Oye, get out of the pond before I come and drag you out," hollered Naveen from the topmost step of the pond.

My unhappiness vanished and I pulled myself out of the pond the next minute.

"You are back. I was waiting for you to return," I said, drying myself with a bath towel.

"Mmm. We need to talk. The others are waiting," said Naveen and strutted off gesturing me to follow.

What? The others were waiting? For what? I just wanted to talk to Arya. Alone, if possible. I didn't want my meddling cousins to be around.

I took my time to change into fresh clothes as I pondered what awaited me at Sree Nilayam. I had a lingering feeling that I was going to be put through some kind of inquiry. Did my actions worry them or something?

Once I entered the living room at Sree Nilayam, I was shocked to see that all of my cousins, their spouses and Ammamma were waiting to pounce on me.

Ammamma looked up, gave me a wide smile and patted the vacant spot next to her on the couch. I had no other option other than to obey her.

"So! Naveen said we were about to discuss something. What are we talking about? Any new announcements? Or plans?" I asked, trying to sound as cheerful as I could.

I might have sounded a little too cheerful because the next moment, Ananya whose BS meter must have gone off snapped at me, "Stop it, will you? How long are you going to pretend that you are not in some kind of trouble? We have been worried sick about you for days now."

"Worried? What for?" I asked, genuinely surprised that I hadn't succeeded in camouflaging my emotions.

"Cut the crap right now. You look like you haven't slept well in days. You don't eat well. You are lost in your thoughts all the time. Do you know how worried I was when I saw you floating in the pond a while ago? I almost jumped in thinking you had done something stupid," snapped Naveen.

"Come on! There is nothing to be worried about, okay. Let's have dinner. I am starving," I said, trying to get up from the sofa.

Ammamma grabbed my wrist. Then she made me sit facing her and addressed me.

"Do you think we can eat calmly without knowing what is bothering you? Look at them. They have been pestering me to talk to you since today morning after you suddenly drove off before sunrise without telling anyone where you were going. Come on, child. We are your family. We want to help you. Is it something with the company? Is there some crisis you are not able to deal with? Are you sick? Did someone hurt you? Please tell us, child. We all are eager to help."

Exhaling deeply, I looked around. Nine pairs of eyes were trained on me, waiting to hear my reply. I could see concern etched clearly on their faces. I felt terrible. As Ammamma said, we were family. I should share my troubles with them. It was time I told them.

"Okay, relax guys. There is nothing wrong at work. And nothing wrong with my health, okay? I will tell you all what is bothering me," I said and took a deep breath to compose myself.

I couldn't even hear anyone breathing as they waited for me to speak. A chuckle escaped from my lips.

I kept my palms on my heart, looked at the loving faces around me and confessed with a smile, "The trouble is that I have fallen in love."

"What?" they all chorused before they all started laughing. Then questions flew at me from all directions.

"Oh my God. Who is that poor girl?" asked Vishal.

"Anyone we know?" asked Arjun.

"Phew! Finally, someone took you down. And how nicely. You can compete for the Devdas award!" exclaimed Kishore.

"What's her name?" That was what was troubling Ananya.

"Is it someone from work?" asked Naveen. "That's what your stars said. That you will find your true love at your workplace."

"Aha! You are wrong for the first time, brother. She is not someone I met through work."

"Whoa. That's a first indeed! Where did you meet her then?" asked Shreya.

"I met her on the day I got lost in the hills," I said, grinning wildly as I waited for my bro-gang to pounce on me.

"You sneaky bastard! Remember how he acted that day? He insisted nothing interesting had happened, when in reality a miracle had occurred. He fell in love! That too with a girl. I was seriously starting to think he was wired differently," said Kishore, clapping on my shoulder.

Ammamma let out a belly laugh. Others were laughing as well.

"Come on, tell us, what is her name?" asked Arya.

"Aathira," I said, looking at Arya pointedly.

"Is she the one you described when Ammamma asked about the kind of girl you wanted as your wife?" asked Shalini, who absorbed facts the fastest among us.

The name together with how I had described her the other day must have rung the bell finally for Arya.

"You mean you love…," she paused, her eyes wide in surprise. Naveen looked at her and the next moment, he also understood who my girl was.

"Wow, you are in love with that girl?" asked Naveen.

"Out with it before I punch you," said Vishal, glowering at me. He clearly didn't appreciate being left out of such a big secret.

I pulled out my phone, browsed through the gallery and found Aathira's close-up from the inter-collegiate dance fest. I handed the phone to Ammamma. She smiled widely as she looked at the photo and patted me on my cheek.

"Wow! She is so pretty. No wonder you fell so hard," exclaimed Shreya, who got the chance to look at it next. My phone was passed next to Kishore, then to Shalini, Ananya, Vishal and then Arjun who were sitting together on one couch.

"You flicked it from the college's Facebook page, didn't you?" said Arya with a chuckle. "I remember this performance. She dances like a dream."

My heart grew warm. She had charmed me with her dance as well.

"Tell me all about her. Arya, is she your student?" asked Ammamma who seemed to have connected the dots.

"Yes, Ammamma. She just completed her engineering this year. She is one of the toppers from her batch. A very good girl. Well-behaved, disciplined, and talented. One of my best students," said Arya.

I felt hugely jealous. Because she knew a lot more about Aathira than me.

"Excellent. Let's bring her into the family then. I will tell Radha the happy news. She will be thrilled," said Ammamma.

I panicked. This was the reason I didn't tell them anything in the first place. One green flag and they would start planning the wedding menu.

"Not yet, Ammamma. The thing is, I love her, but I don't know how she feels about me. In fact, that day in the hills, she refused to be in a serious relationship with me," I said.

The faces around me fell.

"Come on, who can refuse you? A handsome, billionaire CEO proposed to her and she refused? Are you kidding me?" asked Ananya.

"Sadly, that is the truth. Also, she doesn't know I am rich or that I am the CEO of a very successful company. I didn't tell her. All I know about her is her name. I learned she was an alumnus of our college after I checked the dash cam recording from the other day after Arya mentioned the name of her gang of friends. They called themselves the STAR Quartet," I said.

"Okay. I am confused. You act like you have lost the love of your life just because a girl you met briefly rejected you?" asked Naveen. "Is this history repeating all over again?"

Naveen's question shook me. I couldn't find a way to counter it. He was right in a way.

Was this a pattern? Was I obsessed with Aathira because she had rejected me?

"History repeating itself? Is there something you both have not told us?" asked Ananya.

"When he was in college, there was this girl that he liked. When she got engaged to someone else, he behaved the same way as he is doing now. Got drunk, said he would die if he didn't get her and so on."

"No. It is nothing like that. Back then, love was only in my head. Now, I really know I am in love with Aathira. And that she loves me too. She was just scared that day," I said.

Suddenly, all the occupants in the room were looking at me like I had committed some crime.

"Did you harm her in any way?" Arya was the first one to speak. I could feel the anger emanating from her.

"No. I didn't do anything bad to her okay. We clicked from the moment we met. She was alone at home and sad when we met. It was a memorable night," I said.

"You slept with her!" said Vishal. It wasn't even a question. He said that as if he was a hundred per cent sure I had done it.

"Nothing of the sort happened. We just... kissed, okay? That's all," I confessed.

"Just a kiss caused you to behave like this? I tell you, bro, she is the one! I'm speaking from experience," said Kishore. Shreya elbowed him hard in the ribs.

"What? Don't you remember?" asked Kishore quirking his eyebrows.

I smiled but my smile vanished in a blink when I saw Arya's expression. She looked tormented.

"I need to know. Did you kiss her against her wish? Is that why she rejected you?" she asked.

I cringed. But as I looked around, I understood they all had the same doubt.

"Of course not. I didn't force her. It just happened. We talked all night and then at some point, we kissed. That's all. I didn't do anything to scare her or make her feel uncomfortable. Trust me, the kiss we shared was consensual. But the next day morning, she insisted we should forget what happened the previous night. That it was all a mistake," I said.

"And how did you respond?" asked Naveen.

"I didn't want to lose her. How could I? No one has ever made me feel the way she did. I tried to convince her that we should at least be in touch for a while. But she refused to even share her email address. So I walked away that day leaving everything to destiny. Hoping that God will make me meet her again," I said, feeling the need to justify myself in front of everyone I cared for and loved.

"That is sad. Even Nigerian fraudsters have my email address. That was so cruel on her part to not share even her email address," said Kishore.

"Yeah. She could have parted with that easily," said Vishal, agreeing with his brother.

"Whatever, Navneet! She said no. You shouldn't force her. Is that where you rushed to today morning? To plead with her to accept your love?" asked Naveen.

"Yes. But I couldn't meet her. Her family moved homes," I confessed.

"Oh, I am so angry with you. This is giving me deja-vu vibes. I'll repeat it one last time. She said no. That means you should end this obsession. It is time you normalized rejection. Not everyone you like is going to like you back. You can't force love, okay?" snapped Naveen.

His words tore into me like a poisoned arrow, and I felt I couldn't breathe. I got up and walked to the window that opened into the garden that was now bathing in the moonlight and took deep breaths.

I knew why Naveen was being so insistent. The last time I got obsessed over a girl like this, I became the reason Arya and he broke up. All because the girl I had a crush on was also called Arya. It had been such a mess, such a horrible misunderstanding because of the names.

But I was sure of one thing. What I felt for Aathira was nothing like what I felt for my first crush. Then my feelings were conjured by my teenage brain from nothing. With Aathira, what I felt was real. We shared amazing chemistry. Sparks flew when we touched. Our souls merged when our lips collided. She had come alive in my arms that night and our kisses had been explosive, to say the least. Whatever happened in the hills wasn't been one-sided. If we had given it time, our relationship would have bloomed and worked.

But I didn't want to argue with anyone anymore. Anyway, Aathira had vanished from my life yet again. Perhaps, Naveen was right. A no was a no. This time it seemed like a clear no from the universe as well. With Naveen so against it, Arya wouldn't share Aathira's number with me.

My brief love story was indeed over.

I looked around at my family. Were they thinking of me as a weirdo who couldn't handle rejection?

Ananya, Shalini and Shreya were talking to each other in whispers. Arya was suddenly busy checking messages on her phone while her husband had been summoned by Ammamma to occupy the seat I had just vacated. Vishal, Arjun and Kishore were exchanging glances and shrugging as if they didn't know what to say.

My attention was dragged to Arya who had suddenly turned to her gang of girls and was engrossed in a seemingly intense, whispered discussion with them. I had had enough. I didn't even feel hungry anymore. I got up and turned towards the door deciding to go for a long walk in the moonlight.

I needed to clear my head. Maybe Naveen was right. I need to learn to handle rejection.

"Navneet, wait. One minute," said Arya, getting up from the couch and approaching me.

"Naveen might kill me for doing this, but we women think you ought to have another chance. Leena, my friend is asking if she can share my number with Sneha from the STAR Quartet. Three of them are going to be living in Bangalore from now on. One of them, Riddhi is doing an MBA and the other two, Aathira and Trisha got jobs in an MNC there. I can make you and Aathira meet."

Hope glowed bright inside me yet again. I glanced fleetingly at Naveen who was still talking to Ammamma. I didn't want history to repeat in any way. What if my obsession with Aathira hindered her happiness in some way? Also, I didn't want to cause another issue between Naveen and Arya just because I was obsessed with yet another girl. I knew what I had to do.

I pasted a smile on my face. "It's up to you. After all, they are your students. Don't do it for me, though. Naveen is right. It is time I put an end to this obsession," I said.

Arya gave me a blank look for a few seconds as she comprehended what I said but then nodded.

I patted her shoulders and addressed the people I loved most in the universe.

"Listen. I agree with Naveen. It's time I stopped running behind yet another mirage. I have been so blind. But give me some time guys, I promise, I'll bounce back. Now can we eat? I am starving."

⟫⟫⟫

Later, I spent a sleepless night pondering over Naveen's words. The more I thought about it, the more I was convinced that it was all in my head. Just like the last time.

Every thought colluded to reach one conclusion. Aathira didn't like me.

Didn't she push me off that night saying that she heard her mother? Her mother wasn't in the house but Aathira had used her as an excuse to escape from my arms.

Thinking back, I realized I had initiated the kiss. Both times. At night and as well as when we were saying goodbye. No wonder she hadn't wished to prolong our relationship. Aathira must have been disgusted by what I had done. I had tried to take advantage of a helpless, lonely and sad girl.

She was heartbroken over her longtime crush when we met. How had I convinced myself that she would fall in love with me so soon after being burned by something like that?

The tiny ways in which she had responded to me could have been her getting carried away due to a rebound. Or it must have been fear that had made her go still in my arms as I kissed and caressed her.

By morning, I felt like a cad. I felt filthy. When the hymns from the nearby temple wafted into the library that had become my abode during my stay in Sree Nilayam, I got up and took a hot shower.

Then I switched on my Mac and selected the folder I had created for Aathira. My heart squeezed when I pressed the option key together with the command and delete buttons. A window popped up asking if I wanted to permanently delete the selected folder. Without hesitating for even a microsecond, I clicked 'yes.'

Then I logged into my email and dived into all the work that I had neglected because of my obsession.

If Aathira was to be mine, God would make it happen without any conscious effort on my part.

If she was not to be mine, then this was the best that I could do. I had to let her go. To heal a wound, one had to first stop scratching it.

16

Aathira

♡

August 16th, Friday, Bangalore

New hopes, new dreams, new food, new experiences...

Those were our expectations as we stepped out of the interstate train to Bangalore early in the morning. As Riddhi had instructed, we got on the Metro train next to head to our new place in South Bangalore. As the city rushed past us, my first thought was of Navneet. He lived somewhere in this vast city.

Would I run into him unexpectedly again? Maybe right here on this metro train?

What would I do then?

Nothing of the sort happened even though I kept searching for his face everywhere. I was slightly disappointed when we arrived at our destination station before long.

Riddhi came to pick us up at the metro station and we reached our new home in fifteen minutes.

"Wow! This is so cool!" exclaimed Trisha, as we stepped into the apartment. Its minimalistic décor and modern furnishing gave it a very chic look. What pleased Trisha the most was that we had separate bedrooms, with attached bathrooms. The dining and kitchen areas were just to my liking. I could see myself relaxing after work by cooking something delicious in this kitchen with adequate pantry, storage, cooking, sink and preparation areas.

"Don't you think this is a hundred per cent upgrade to our room in the hostel?" said Riddhi as she flopped into the couch in the living room.

The climate was cool and it felt as if I was back in the hills. And then I remembered that Bangalore was located 3000 feet above sea level.

"Oh my God, this is my favourite spot in the whole house," exclaimed Trisha as she stepped into the balcony. I joined her along with Ridhi. The night view of Bangalore with its sparkling neon signs, lit windows, and the star-spangled horizon from the 12th floor of this residential complex was captivating indeed.

"I agree. This view is just priceless," I said, taking in the splendid view of the city that was to be our home from now on.

"You see that building there with that giant shining globe? That is the main block of the Technopark where your company is located. My campus is not visible from here. It is on the other side," explained Riddhi who had moved in a week ago.

"This apartment is very convenient. We have a supermarket inside the complex together with other amenities such as the gym, clubhouse and pool. I will take you around tomorrow morning. My father did a great job finding this apartment in such a short time. The previous owner was a former client of his who has now migrated to Canada," said Riddhi.

We quickly decided that I was to have the bedroom previously designed for the teenage daughter of the family. Thankfully it was not all pink as I had thought it would be but aesthetically designed with one wall covered with a mural of cherry blossoms. I loved the room on sight.

Trisha's room had a black wall, which she declared she was going to decorate with a photo collage of her favourite Korean stars.

"Riddhi, your room has a balcony as well. Nice! Oh, I forgot. That girl is going to bite our heads off if we don't give her a video tour of the house," said Trisha reminding us of the promise we made to Sneha.

Sneha looked glum maybe owing to the new guy who had come to meet her today. When was she going to say no to her parents? Weren't they seeing how miserable she was?

"I am so jealous. I am going to visit you all next month. I am applying for jobs online. If all goes well, I will be able to join you girls," said Sneha once Trisha ended the video tour.

We were all tired to the bone. We took a quick shower after dumping our bags and suitcases into our respective rooms. Then clad in our pyjamas, we climbed into Riddhi's bed and talked ourselves to sleep.

In the next two days, Riddhi took us around in her car. Her father had provided her with a driver as well. The driver, Manjunath, was a middle-aged man with silver hair who communicated with us in sketchy English. He told us about the history of the places, the best tourist spots, and the best restaurants and eateries as he drove us around.

I was liking how green Bangalore was even though it was a bustling metropolitan city. After every kilometre, we came across parks and lakes. Most of the roads were lined by trees. But there were cons too. We did pass slums, narrow, crowded streets, waste dumping grounds that stank like rotten meat, open sewers and bumper-to-bumper traffic that moved at a snail's pace.

According to Manjunath, the area we were staying in was one of the well-developed municipalities in Bangalore.

"You can survive here without learning Kannada. But if you learn Kannada, this place will feel like home," explained Manjunath. "I am not a native of Karnataka. I migrated here from Andhra Pradesh two decades ago. Now Bengaluru feels more like home than my native place."

I noticed how he never called it Bangalore. It was always Bengaluru.

"If you call it Bangalore, it might offend the sentiments of the natives," he said when Trisha asked him for the reason.

Then he told us the story of how the place was originally called *'Benda-kaalu-ooru'* (the place of boiled beans). Incidentally, Kempe Gowda, a chieftain under the Vijayanagara Empire, got lost in the forest when he was out hunting. The starving man was fed with boiled beans by an old lady. To honour the memory, he named the city he founded at the place Benda-kaalu-uru. The name later metamorphosed into Bengaluru. Another theory was that Kempe Gowda's mother was originally from old Bengaluru and he named the city in her honour. The British captured the city after defeating Tipu Sultan and called it Bangalore for ease and it remained that way till 2006 when the name was officially changed back to Bengaluru.

"What did you feed your dog whisperer when he came to your house?" asked Riddhi, when we stepped out of the car to explore Lalbagh, a well-maintained and pretty botanical garden in urban Bangalore.

"Uppumanga Chammandhi," I said. I had an inkling why she had asked.

"Thank God, he isn't a King. Else, he would have renamed that hill Uppumanga-uru, or even better, Chammandi-uru," said Trisha with a chuckle. Riddhi snickered.

"You guys! I also fed him rice, egg curry and potato *mezhukkupuratti*. And a cheese sandwich for breakfast. Try all the name combinations for my place," I egged them on.

The girls took the bait and my ears were aching like hell by the time we got back home.

We had our dinner outside. So after bathing, we watched a mystery thriller K-Drama on Netflix at Trisha's insistence. My eyes hurt trying to read the subtitles to understand what was happening. I pleaded to be excused from the torture and picked up a novel. Trisha didn't even need subtitles! When Riddhi tried to escape as well, Trisha threatened to kill her. So, our hapless landlord fell asleep on the couch itself.

Sunday was spent unpacking and organizing our stuff. As we were to start our training at QIS the next day, we went to sleep early. Riddhi had asked Manjunath to pick up and drop us at the company on day one. From what the HR guy at QIS had told us, there was a pickup and drop facility for our area that we could avail of once we completed the formalities required by the accounting department.

***

Quarks Info Solutions —QIS— was located inside the Technopark with various other software giants. Located in South Bangalore, the Technopark boasted of tranquillity being away from the hustle and bustle. Giant palms lined the roads that led into the various blocks. Beautiful landscapes, amazing buildings and software professionals hustling about were everywhere.

When we entered the road that Google said led into the interior of the park, a white BMW passed us. My heart skipped a beat. Immediately, Trisha elbowed me in the ribs and Riddhi turned to look at me from the front passenger's seat.

I rolled my eyes.

"It seems like your Navneet works here too!" exclaimed Trisha.

"It might not be his car," I tried saying, even though it did seem like the car I had seen the other day.

"I am hundred per cent sure, it is the same car. Oh my God, I have to ask around as soon as I meet the others in the company. And make our Laila-Majnu meet!" declared Trisha, hugging me tightly. I swatted her arm.

"Shut up. You will do no such thing. And I heard there are about a hundred companies in here. It might take us years to find him. That is if he does work here," I said.

"I wonder why Arya Ma'am didn't text me. I had asked Sneha to give her my number," said Trisha.

"She might not want to meet us, what else?" asked Riddhi.

I sighed absentmindedly, as my mind had entered into a vortex of thoughts featuring Navneet. I was nervous for no reason. But the other two immediately turned and smiled at me.

"Believe in the signs, girl," said Riddhi.

"God definitely has plans for you both," said Trisha.

I ignored them and focused on smoothing out the ruffles on my white Anarkali churidar. For some reason, my heart continued to race as we entered the building tower occupied by QIS. It was eight floors high and our training was happening on the second floor.

The receptionist guided us to the lift marked employees only and asked us to meet Miss Chaturvedi at the second-floor reception, who was in charge of the training. We pressed the call button on the lift and waited for it to arrive along with a few others.

My phone pinged with a message from Riddhi. While I was answering her, two men dressed in suits, one in black and the other in grey, passed by us seemingly engrossed in some serious discussion. They entered the lift that was reserved for executives at the other end of the corridor. I casually observed the two men. I staggered because the man dressed in black seemed looked achingly familiar. It couldn't be!

Just as the lift doors were closing, the man wearing the black suit looked up and our eyes met for a few brief seconds. Navneet!

Stunned by the cognizance, I grabbed Trisha's arm to steady myself.

"What happened? You look so pale. Is everything okay?" asked Trisha.

"Nothing. I am okay!" I mumbled.

My eyes wandered to the executive lift again. Before I could see which floor their lift stopped, our lift arrived and Trisha pulled me into it.

"I think I just saw Navneet," I said, blowing out a breath I didn't know I was holding.

"What? Where? When?" asked Trisha, looking around.

"The guy in the black suit who went into that executive lift, it was Navneet," I said, still dazed by the fact that I had seen him.

"Shit. I was looking at the other guy. He looked almost like Korean actor Lee Min-ho," said Trisha. "This is so amazing, darling. God definitely has plans. Maybe he is an executive in this company. Daebak!"

I didn't say anything. Because my thoughts were running in a different direction altogether. Navneet did not show any signs of recognition when our eyes met. Even though it was brief, I recognised him. Then why hadn't he?

Had he forgotten me already?

Were the memories of that night no longer significant to him?

My heart squeezed painfully because he hadn't given me a reason to hope.

17
Navneet

"Give me a moment. I need to use the washroom," I said, as soon as we entered my corner office.

I hadn't heard a word of what Rohit had spoken after seeing the girl who resembled Aathira in the crowded corridor. My first impulse had been to stop the lift door from closing and check if it was her. But it had been too late. As the lift moved up, I tried to listen to Rohit. Nothing registered. It was as if someone had knocked me out.

I hurried to the washroom and splashed cold water over my face repeatedly till a semblance of normalcy returned. I had become like a drug addict dealing with withdrawal symptoms. I wasn't even sure if it was Aathira. It could have been her. Our eyes had met briefly, leaving me confused. She hadn't smiled or waved at me. If it had been Aathira, she wouldn't have acted like a stranger. Maybe it was her white dress and dark curls which had made me think it was my girl from the hills.

The vision of her dressed in white, her hair loose, and dancing around the fire was indelibly imprinted in my memory. A random stranger dressed similarly was making me lose my composure. It was time I consulted a counsellor.

I really needed help. It was time I stopped obsessing over someone who didn't even like me.

Rohit was waiting for me, spinning a pen between his fingers. A habit he had when he was either bored or anxious.

"You, alright?" asked Rohit, giving me a concerned look.

"Perfectly alright. So, let's run through the presentation one more time before the client logs in."

The call with our Dubai client lasted for an hour and a half. Just as he was about to leave, Rohit paused at the door.

"Are you sure you don't want to meet the newbies? They'd surely want to meet the CEO and get inspired," he said.

"I am sure my COO will inspire them enough. If I wrap my work in time, I will come down and see you guys. But the chances are very low." I had a mountain of pending tasks that demanded my attention.

"Okay then, I will leave you to your problem pile," he said, gesturing to the stack of files I had to go through.

As soon as Rohit left, I dived into the day's work. I reviewed and approved new project budgets and ideas, and then answered my emails.

I waited for Rohit to return after his meet and greet session with the new trainees so that we could leave together for the lunch meeting with a prospective client.

A local supermarket chain in Bangalore wanted an app created exclusively for them. They wanted to enable their customers to shop from their various outlets from the convenience of their homes. Since they were new to the whole app thing, the owner wanted to meet us to discuss ideas and the viability of the project. Since the man was Rohit's family friend, a lunch meeting had been scheduled at the Ritz-Carlton in Bangalore.

As Rohit and I stepped out of the executive lift, discussing the project details, a group came out of the employee lift. The same girl I had seen in the morning appeared before me with two others. She was laughing at something one of the other girls said and I froze. My heart hadn't screamed 'halt' for no reason in the morning. It was Aathira indeed.

Happiness filled my entire being. I stood rooted to the spot and stared after her as she walked towards the staff canteen located on the ground floor of the adjacent building.

"Cat got your tongue? This is the second time you have gone all silent on me today," said Rohit, walking back to me and clapping my shoulder. "So, out with it now. What is it?"

I felt like a kid who had been handed a box of his favourite chocolates. Destiny had thrown the ball back into my court. Was she an employee in my company?

I grinned at him. He raised one eyebrow.

"Do you see that girl dressed in white?" I asked him, pointing at Aathira.

"That newbie with the curly hair?" asked Rohit. "She is hot and exactly my type. Met her today morning. She is smart."

I had an insane urge to smash his aristocratic nose. "Don't even dare to look at her. She is mine."

Rohit scoffed. "Yours? I have at least met her once. And you haven't. Don't you think it is too early to make such claims," he said.

"I've met her before you. Remember my girl from the hills? That's her."

"Whoa! You mean she is the girl who rejected you? I like it. I am definitely more interested in her right now," teased Rohit.

I punched his shoulder and we walked to the parking lot bantering. Rohit paused and gestured toward the group.

"You might have to stake your claim soon. See that guy in blue who is accompanying her? He could be a prospective rival. He has stuck to her side like superglue since morning. Looks smitten. They are from our college. Every time she spoke at the meet and greet today, he clapped the loudest."

I eyed the guy Rohit had pointed out. The trio had found a table in the outdoor area of the canteen. Jealousy coiled and hissed inside me like an anaconda as I watched the guy pull out a chair for Aathira. She smiled at him as she sat and he slipped into the chair next to her.

"What is his name?" I asked.

"Diju, if I remember right," said Rohit.

"Let Diju try. She is going to be mine. I am going to court her. This time, I will try my best to convince her that I might just die if she rejects me again," I said.

After looking at her with longing one last time, I joined Rohit and stepped into my car.

When we passed by the canteen on our way out, my eyes automatically sought Aathira. I didn't like that the guy with her was leaning so close to her. My fists clenched and I had all the mind to drag him into an arena and punch him till he looked a bloody mess.

"Stop," I almost screamed at the driver. The driver applied the brakes abruptly and the car screeched to a stop a few metres away from the canteen.

Rohit raised an eyebrow. "What now?" he demanded.

"Time to scare my rival and claim my girl," I declared, as I stepped out of the car.

"We don't have the time for that now," protested Rohit. I ignored him and approached my girl even as my heart thudded like crazy against my ribs.

Aathira saw me only when I was a meter away from their table. Her eyes opened wide and her delectable lips formed a shapely O.

"Hey, Aathira! What a pleasant surprise. Is it really you?" I asked as I stopped by their table.

"Hey, Navneet!" she said and stood up to greet me. She just kept looking at me as if she couldn't quite believe that it was me.

"It's so nice to meet you again. Where do you work?" I asked as if I didn't know.

"At Quarks Info Solutions. And you?" she asked.

"That's awesome. I work at QIS too. See, we met again. I guess destiny has spoken, don't you agree?" I said, and she looked at me with a coy smile. My whole body buzzed with the desire to pull her into my arms and kiss her in front of everyone. With extreme effort, I controlled myself and grinned at her.

"This is my friend Trisha and this is Diju, another college mate. Guys, meet Navneet."

The guy Diju got up, searched my face and, as he offered his hand to shake, he asked, "By any chance, do you happen to be *the* Navneet Chandran?"

I smiled at him as I shook his hand. "Yup. The very one."

"Wow! So wonderful to meet you, sir. You are an inspiration!" said Diju, literally whooping with joy.

I smiled warmly at him, immediately deciding to forgive him for flirting with Aathira. He had redeemed himself in my eyes with his correctly timed words.

It was clear to me that Aathira and her friend had no idea who I was. Her friend was eying me with newfound interest. It was better to let her find out on her own. Diju would surely tell them who I was. I would have loved to see her reaction to that piece of news, but I was running late for my meeting.

"Have to rush, guys. See you very soon, Aathira," I said as a parting shot, devouring her with my eyes one last time. My heart rejoiced when she blushed.

I walked away from the trio holding my head high and with a goofy grin.

"You look smug, like a dog that just peed to mark its territory," said Rohit as I stepped into the car.

I chuckled. "You got me wrong. I am the alpha wolf. Not a dog," I said, wriggling my eyebrows.

Rohit snorted.

"Nay. You are a puppy. See how you are drooling!" he said.

I leaned back in the car seat and closed my eyes. My heart was at ease once again. My would-be queen was right where she belonged: inside my empire, under my protection.

18
Aathira

Did that really happen? I wondered as I watched Navneet's car drive away. My eyes darted to Trisha and she made the Korean finger heart using her thumb and index finger. My pulse was still racing.

"You guys are friends with *the* Navneet Chandran! When did that happen?"

"*The* Navneet Chandran? Is he someone famous?" asked Trisha, voicing my doubt as well.

Diju, who was quite the news source when it came to the IT field, gazed at us as if we were nincompoops.

"How can you not know him? He was celebrated by newspapers just a year ago when his app was bought by an American billionaire for 600 million dollars. He is an alumnus of our college and, more importantly, he is the CEO and founder of QIS!"

I gaped at Trisha whose eyes had gone wide as saucers. I was sure mine looked the same.

"I might just pass out," said Trisha, fanning herself with her fingers.

"Didn't you know that?" Diju asked me. "He behaved as if you two were close."

"He is an acquaintance. But I didn't know where he worked and all…," I managed.

"But still! He is like a legend in our college. Almost all of us guys want to become like him one day. The guy is like our own Mark Zuckerburg. He founded QIS just five years ago as a one-man company and see how famous it already is! It employs thousands of young engineers at its three branches in Mumbai, Delhi and Bangalore. They have an overseas branch in Dubai and I've heard they are contemplating opening a branch in South Korea."

"South Korea? Daebak!" exclaimed Trisha. Then she whispered in my ears. "Aathira darling, do tell Navneet to transfer me to South Korea when they open the branch there."

I stomped on her feet. She moaned.

Diju was in no mood to stop.

"I think the expansion to South Korea came up because his partner Rohit is half-Korean. His mother was the daughter of a rich South Korean businessman. His father fell in love with his mother while he worked in South Korea and the two eloped and got married in India. Her parents didn't approve of the marriage even after her death. I think it was only this year that her father came to India to meet his only heir, his long-lost grandson. I heard he proposed to open a branch in Seoul as compensation for the lost years."

"No wonder he looks like Lee Min-ho. Does he speak Korean as well?" asked Trisha.

Diju continued to bombard Trisha with all the information he had on the COO of QIS, Rohit Varma.

Trisha was absorbing every bit of information like her life depended on it. I was quite sure that Mr Rohit Varma had suddenly become her 'Oppa'!

"Close your mouth. A fly might make a home right in that hole in your molar," I teased Trisha. She shrugged and ignored me.

Our lunch arrived just then and I dug into my food with a happy and content heart. Vegetable *pulav* had never tasted as good as it did now.

The rest of the day passed in a happy trance as I ruminated about one special person. Every other minute, I expected he might walk into our training room. When we had about an hour remaining in the work day, we were all taken on a tour of the company, to show us the various departments, and the recreation areas. The last stop was on the top floor which had the offices of the bosses and the finance department.

My heart thudded as we passed by the CEO's room. But he didn't seem to be around. After showing us around the finance department, the group was dismissed. It was 5 PM already and we were told we could go home.

Just as we were waiting near the elevators, the executive's lift at the other end of the floor opened and Navneet came out with the same person he was with earlier. My heart started racing at an annoying speed.

His voice sounded deeper and more mesmerizing than I remembered when I heard him call my name.

"Hey! I guess you are done for the day," he said, approaching us.

"Yes. We just finished a tour of all the departments," I said, trying to remain composed.

"Okay. Superb. By the way, this is my best friend and business partner Rohit Varma. Rohit, meet Aathira and her friend, Trisha."

"Hi, girls. Nice meeting you. You are prettier in person, Aathira. Navneet cannot stop talking about you," said Rohit.

Navneet whispered something in his ears.

Interesting. *I looked better in person?* Where did he see my photo?

Rohit chuckled aloud hearing Navneet's whispered response and then addressed me, "Okay, before I get myself killed, I will take off. So bye."

"Ignore him. He loves to blabber," said Navneet.

Rohit raised his eyebrows dramatically, smiled at us once again and walked to an office reserved for the COO of QIS.

When I looked at Navneet he raked his fingers through his hair, shrugged and grinned at me. Questions, hundreds of them, were burning inside me.

"Aathira, I was wondering if I could talk to you for a moment. Privately. Can we?"

I looked at Trisha, confused as to what to do.

"I need to use the washroom. You guys go ahead. I will meet you here in another fifteen minutes."

After directing Trisha toward the restroom, Navneet guided me to his office.

His office was as large as the training room we had been in all day. It was a medium-sized seminar room that accommodated twenty new trainees along with their respective tables. He directed me to a couch at the other end of the room that seemed perfect for small business meetings or to just relax with a cup of coffee.

"What would you like? Tea or coffee?" he asked.

"Coffee," I said.

He walked into an inner room and minutes later, the aroma of coffee wafted outside. Maybe there was a pantry in there. I took the time to look around. The first thing that caught my eye was the beautifully designed white bookshelf behind his desk, filled mostly with technical books. The central portion of the shelf was designed differently and held a few trophies, a 3D design of the company logo and some other decor pieces. Most of the furniture was done in white. The wall next to the sofa I was sitting on was completely glass-panelled giving me a beautiful bird's eye view of Bangalore.

Navneet returned bearing two cups of hot coffee.

"So, how have you been?" he asked, sitting on the chair opposite the couch.

"I am good," I said and gazed back at him in wonder. He looked so different from the person I had met that night yet somehow very familiar.

Navneet's eyes searched my face for a full minute. He got up and stood near the glass wall, looking outside. Then he turned and looked at me. He appeared agitated.

"I haven't been able to stop thinking about you, Aathira. In the past two weeks, I haven't been my normal self because I missed you like crazy, so much that even my family got worried. It was like we were separated after being in love for several years. I went back to your place, you know, in search of you. But your family had moved. After struggling with my obsession with you, and not finding a way to meet you, I almost shelved my dreams of being with you with great difficulty. And now here you are. Don't you think destiny wants us to be together?" he asked.

I felt warm all over. He had occupied my thoughts every second in the past few weeks too. But was it prudent to say that to my new boss? There were boundaries one shouldn't cross and this certainly was one of those. I suddenly felt awkward.

"The person I met that day in the hills and the person I met today seem entirely different. I am confused. I really don't know what to say," I said.

"Did you like me that night in the hills?" he asked softly.

"Yes, I did," I said.

"Did you hate me when we met today?" he asked, taking a step closer.

"I didn't say that. But you are my boss. That changes things," I said.

"Me being your boss changes nothing. I fell in love with you that night without knowing anything about you. We didn't talk about this stuff. I loved the person you were. I could talk with you for hours. You made me forget all my worries. You made my world come alive. I am crazy about you. Do you know that? Did you even think about me afterwards?" he asked.

I looked at him and the intensity in his eyes and the sincerity in his words moved me.

"Would you believe it if I told you that I have thought about you every single day since then? After we said goodbye that day, I hoped you would look back and return to me. It broke my heart when you just left without looking back. Your memories hound me 24/7. I see your name everywhere. I cannot seem to stop thinking about you. Did you know that I almost met you twice after that?"

"Twice? I know I missed you at the college campus. Did you see me anywhere after that?" he asked.

I smiled at him. "You have actually met my parents," I said. He tilted his head and narrowed his eyes.

"When? How?" he asked.

"Do you remember the small roadside restaurant you drank tea from when you visited Wayanad last week? Iyappan's Family Restaurant? Iyappan is my father. My mother was at the cash counter that day," I said.

"Oh my God. I didn't even look at them properly. I was totally down in the dumps then. I might have come off as a pretentious prick," he said.

"Sheru was barking his head off to grab your attention. He was locked in my room. I saw you only when you were getting into your car. He was so sad when you drove off," I recounted.

"I know he loves me. Not so sure about his human, though," he said and pouted.

I chuckled.

He came and sat next to me on the couch. Gently, he took my hands in his and gazed straight into my eyes.

"I love you like crazy. Do you even like me?"

How could he ask me that? Did he believe that I didn't care for him? I decided to tease him a bit.

"Come on, I don't really know you. I surely didn't fall in love with a billionaire CEO. I am in love with someone else," I said, looking into his eyes.

"So you don't love me?" He looked crestfallen.

He let go of my hands and was about to move away when I clutched his arm. "Ask me who I love," I said softly, urging him to sit back near me.

"Who do you love?" he asked, his eyes a pool of sadness.

"My dog-whisperer," I said.

His face lit up with a smile. He leaned closer and cupped my cheek, pressing his forehead to mine.

"Thank God you didn't say another guy's name. I might have ended up murdering him," he whispered, and I snorted.

He stared and smiled at me for a few seconds. Then his lips descended to mine in a tender kiss. I loved it when he pulled me to his lap to deepen the kiss. I loved how his hands raked through my hair. I loved the way he crushed me to him. I loved every single second of our togetherness. I wrapped my hands around his neck and kissed him back with all the love I felt in my heart. My dog-whisperer, my secret lover, my employer, my new boss — was kissing me again. And what a hot kiss it was turning to be. Tender and yet passionate, filled with promises for so much more.

"We should stop, darling. Else, I might break a hundred company rules," he said. "Besides, we can meet again later tonight if you agree."

"Tonight? How? Where?"

"Being your boss has its perks, you see. I just found out from HR that we live in the same apartment complex. Just a different block. If I am not asking too much, can I invite you to meet my family? We are having a dinner party tonight. Nothing big, just family. Will you come?"

Wouldn't meeting his family mean he wanted to take our relationship one notch higher? Happiness burst like festival crackers in my heart.

"How can I? Isn't this too early?" I asked even though I wholeheartedly wanted to go.

"If you feel awkward coming alone, bring your friends with you. I want you to meet my cousins. They are leaving Bangalore in a few days and they do want to meet you."

Did that mean that he had already told them about me? When?

"Okay. Can I confirm after I ask my friends?"

Just then, a knock sounded at the door. The door opened a crack, and Trisha's head appeared.

"Can I come in?"

"Please come in, Trisha. Would you like a coffee?"Navneet asked.

"No. I am afraid we have to leave. Our driver just called me. He is waiting for us at the entrance."

"Oh, okay. Hopefully, we will meet again later today. Aathira will fill you in," said Navneet.

Trisha looked at me and wriggled her eyebrows. I mouthed 'Later.'

Navneet walked us to the executive lift and entered the passcode to let us in. The lift was bigger and majestic looking compared to the ones for the employees. Once the lift doors closed, Trisha pounced on me.

"You guys made out on that couch, right?" she asked.

"Shut up, we didn't," I said, but a blush crept up my face.

"Liar, liar pants on fire! Your lips totally give you away. They look swollen like plums right now. And look at your dress! It looks delightfully crumpled," she said. "Oh, I can't wait to tell the others. This is a scandal."

"I will kill you!" I knew already though that my warning didn't mean a thing to her.

We walked out of the company and found Manjunath waiting at the entrance.

"Let's call the girls now and tell them," screamed Trisha pulling out her mobile, the second we stepped into the car.

"Wait, girl. First, let's reach home," I said grabbing her phone and gesturing at Manjunath.

Was she going to out all my secrets in front of a stranger?

"Okay. Then let me text them."

"Patience, Trisha!" I tried one more time.

She scooted to the other end of the car seat and started typing furiously. Her thumbs flew over the keypad. The next minute, her message popped up in our group chat.

Trisha: GIRLS… BREAKING NEWS! Get ready for a group call at 6. Make sure not to miss this one.

Riddhi: Where are you, girls? Are you okay? Didn't you meet Manjunath?

Trisha: Relax. We are on the way back home. You won't believe who we met today!

I rolled my eyes. Trisha was not going to last till 6 o clock. She looked like she'd burst if she didn't tell the girls about Navneet.

Sneha: Who?

Trisha: Won't say. Wait till six. I want to see the expressions on your faces when I break the news.

Riddhi: Aathira, did she meet some Korean at the company? Is that why she is freaking out?

Trisha: Why are you asking her? She won't say anything. I am the one with the daebak news.

Sneha: *searching eyes emoji*

Riddhi: *face with tongue stuck-out emoji*

Trisha closed WhatsApp and grinned at me.

"Should I tell them now?" she asked.

"Don't," I said knowing how much difficult it was for her to keep her mouth shut.

Rushing home, Trisha revealed everything to Riddhi who kept whooping in delight at Trisha's timely revelations starting from who we met in the afternoon and ending with my scandalous meeting with my boss in his office. Yeah, she didn't last till six.

I then told them about Navneet's invitation.

"Meeting family, huh? Things are progressing super fast indeed," said Trisha, giving me a double thumbs up.

I gave her a tight hug.

"Where does he live?" asked Riddhi.

"Guess!" I said.

"Don't tell me!" she said, guessing the answer correctly.

"God is definitely on your team. Worry nothing, my dear! You are in safe hands," said Trisha.

"Let's go. His family means Arya Ma'am will be there too. We already have company. Call him and tell him we are coming," said Riddhi.

I hugged her and Trisha too joined in.

"Look at her! She is behaving as if we gave her permission to marry him," said Trisha.

"As if," I protested.

"Go call him," said Riddhi, patting my shoulder.

Navneet sounded thrilled when I told him that the girls had said yes to attending the party.

"Texted you my address. I'll be waiting for you. Don't make me wait for too long though," said Navneet before hanging up.

"They live in block one. Ours is block three, right?" I asked Riddhi, checking his apartment address.

"Block one? That block consists only of luxury apartments. I've heard some of the residents have converted an entire floor into one single apartment," she said.

"Where do you get such info from?" I asked. Riddhi had become an expert about everything concerning our place and Bangalore in general within the one week she had been here. Her speciality was that she could talk with anyone and everyone to get the information she needed.

"Oh, the maid who comes to clean likes to talk," said Riddhi.

"Pssh. One single apartment covering an entire floor? Each floor has six flats here, right?" Trisha asked.

"Yup. That is what she said. They buy an entire floor directly during the construction and modify it to suit their needs. The penthouse there is amazing according to her," said Riddhi.

"I wonder what our boss's apartment looks like," said Trisha.

Just then a message pinged in the group chat.

Sneha: No group call? It's six already.

"Trisha, you just forgot about your grand revelation!" said Riddhi with a chuckle.

"Girls, please act surprised. Else poor Sneha will feel so bad," said Trisha, as she pressed the group video call button.

Riddhi managed to act totally surprised and I looked bashful enough to make Sneha go 'ooh' and 'aah', and clap her hands in glee.

"I am so jealous. If possible, video call me from the party, Trisha. I think I am suffering from major FOMO here," said Sneha with a pout.

"I will," promised Trisha. "Now let's get ready girls. We have an impression to make at our boss's private party."

"Help! What should I wear?" I asked thinking about my very ordinary wardrobe.

Trisha and Riddhi looked at each other and then at me. Of course, my question surprised them. I was not someone who fussed over clothes. That was the one question they would have never expected me to ask. But, today, I was desperate to impress the man I loved.

"You should consider going in your birthday suit. He might appreciate it more," said Trisha.

"Shut. Up!" I snapped at her.

"Yeah. That's really a good idea," seconded Riddhi.

Both of them laughed aloud. They were having so much fun vexing me.

"Girls, be serious," I pleaded.

"Wear that cobalt-blue *Anarkali* that you wore for the inter-collegiate dance fest. That suits you the best," said Riddhi.

Did I even have it with me? After getting it dry cleaned after the performance, I hadn't taken it out of its cover. It was a birthday gift from the trio. If I had it, it would be the best choice. Simple, elegant and comfortable. Luckily, when

I checked my cupboard, I found it tucked at the bottom of the cupboard beneath the only silk sari I owned. I had kept these two in my luggage as an afterthought considering situations just like the one we were facing now.

"Girls, I think I will wear this. I am off to take a bath," I declared to the duo before heading into the bathroom.

I took my time to wash off the tiredness of the day, lathering myself with my lavender-scented soap. Like usual, I applied a lavish coat of moisturizing lotion and lip balm right after getting out of the bathroom. Bangalore's climate was similar to the climate back home and could be harsh on my skin. My lips were especially very sensitive and cracked at the first sign of dryness.

After blow-drying my hair, I set them into waves using Riddhi's curling iron. I decided to go with a minimum makeup look and only lined my eyes with kajal and applied nude lip colour. Thankfully, my face was blemish-free and shone just with the moisturizer itself. And I didn't want to look like I tried too hard, did I?

Once ready, I joined the others.

"Wow, darling. You look like a million bucks. Your dog-whisperer might fall on his knees and beg you to marry him," said Trisha, giving me a warm hug.

"Yes. Effortlessly beautiful. That's how you look," said Riddhi.

I smiled. If one had friends like these, one would never feel any insecurity of any sort. They were far more beautiful than I was. Their outfits were costlier and they normally used the best make-up brands. I used the ones I got from the supermarket and my sense of fashion was inferior to theirs. Yet, they never said a disparaging word even once. They shared what was theirs with me anytime they felt I lacked anything without me uttering a single word. Wasn't

I lucky to have such great friends?

At seven-thirty, Navneet called.

"Are you girls ready?" he asked.

"Yeah, we are on our way. Is there a change in plan?" I asked wondering why he had called.

"No. No change in plans. I will wait for you in the apartment lobby then. Can't wait to see you," he said.

The excitement in his voice washed over me and I couldn't help but smile like a giddy teenager.

"Okay, let's go before she melts and becomes mush," teased Trisha.

Block number one had a different ambience altogether, starting right from the landscaping in front of the building. The lobby looked like it belonged in a star hotel. Trisha let out a low whistle as she took in the chandeliers and the marble mosaic paintings lining the walls. There was a fountain at the centre of the lobby and Navneet was waiting for us right there. He grinned and waved when he saw us. My pulse raced like a Maglev train. He was dressed in a V-necked white sweater and jeans, paired with white sneakers.

"Did we make you wait?" I asked. The walk here had taken us longer than expected.

"No. I just came down. Thanks for coming, Trisha and ...," he paused, looking at Riddhi.

"Riddhi. Nice to meet you," said Riddhi.

"Ah, the R in the STAR quartet," said Naveen.

"You know about us?" asked Trisha, eyeing me.

"Of course. Your friend here told me about you all. And yeah, my sister-in-law too had only praises for you girls," said Navneet.

"Thank God!" chorused the two and we all laughed together.

Navneet led us to the elevator and guided us in. When he pressed the button to the penthouse, Trisha and Riddhi exchanged glances and then looked at me. Navneet leaned against the back of the lift and I stood next to him. Trisha and Riddhi helpfully moved to the front as if determined to give us privacy.

"You look beautiful," Navneet whispered in my ear.

"Thank you," I whispered back, and blood rushed to my cheeks as our eyes met.

The heat of his gaze, his delicious scent and his nearness made the air between us sizzle. I wondered if Trisha and Riddhi felt the heat from our bodies.

"Are you nervous?" he asked.

"A little," I admitted.

"Don't be. They are all eager to meet you," he said, taking my hand in his. He weaved his fingers through mine and warmth coursed through me. He raised my hand to his lips and gently kissed it before he wound his other hand around my hips. I felt safe, happy and content.

The elevator door pinged open at the topmost floor and Navneet guided us out, his hand placed gently against the small of my back. My whole body burned with longing as heat spread from his palm to everywhere in my body. I wished to sink into his arms. I badly needed a hug. From him.

Navneet pressed the doorbell and Arya Ma'am opened the door with a wide smile.

"I cannot tell you how happy I am to meet you all," she said, welcoming each of us with a hug.

We stepped into the living room and I forgot to breathe. I could hear whispers of amazement from Trisha and Riddhi too.

It was as if we had stepped into a palace. The living room was wide, spacious and breathtakingly beautiful. Everything was either white or gold. White walls with panels of gold. Curtains and doors in white. Gold ornate vases with white flowers. The couches were white but the throw pillows were all gold. The central rug was made of white fur. The round coffee table had a mirror finish that magnified the beauty of everything around.

While the house mesmerized us, I knew we were being closely scrutinized by the group of women sitting inside the room.

I smiled nervously at them.

"So, ladies, meet Aathira, my girl from the hills. And, I can now tell you for sure that she doesn't hate me," declared Navneet, stepping closer to me and slipping an arm around me possessively.

Every single face in the room split wide with a smile. Not one face had a frown. Standing in front of them, I couldn't help but blush.

Yet, for some strange reason, I felt even more nervous.

They all looked like sophisticated people. I wondered what Navneet had told them about me. I wondered how they would react when they heard about my life situation.

These people seemed to live in a world very different from mine. A single glance at their home had made that clear to me.

My parents worked hard to earn a living. I wondered if these women had ever experienced poverty. Was I building a sky castle that was going to crash any moment?

Did I even deserve to be loved by a guy like Navneet?

From what I could see, he could get any girl he wanted. Yes, he showed enough signs to convince me he loved me. But would it last?

When he truly knew me as a person, won't he find I lacked so much?

I wasn't as brilliant and beautiful as Arya Ma'am. I wasn't as good-looking as the pretty woman with grey eyes smiling at me. I didn't look as gorgeous as the dusky beauty who was bouncing a baby on her lap. And the old lady sitting next to her looked vaguely familiar. I gasped when I recognised her. Arundhati Mukundan?

I turned to Navneet who was smiling warmly at me.

Was this a dream?

19

Navneet

"Aathira, let me introduce you to my most favourite person in this whole universe," I said, leading a seemingly overwhelmed Aathira to the couch where Ammamma was seated, along with Ananya and Shalini. "This is our sweet grandmother, the great Arundhathi Mukundan. She is an author. I guess you already know her."

"Yes, I do," she said breathily as she smiled at Ammamma. "I have read all of your books and I am a huge fan."

"Come here, sweetheart. I have been waiting to see you. We all have been," said Ammamma, urging Aathira to join her on the couch.

Aathira looked extremely nervous as she sat next to Ammamma. Ananya welcomed her with a hug. Shalini leaned forward and said hello. I watched fondly as they introduced themselves to Aathira and made small talk.

When I continued to stand there, Ananya turned to me and narrowed her eyes at me.

"You don't have to stand here like her bodyguard. We won't eat her up. Go and help Naveen and Vishal in the kitchen. We want to talk to your girl for a bit," said Ananya.

"Okay, okay! But why are they still in there? I told you it wasn't a good idea to allow the cook to take the day off. We might have to order in very soon," I said, looking in the direction of the kitchen.

My dear brother and Vishal had taken it upon themselves to feed us tonight after dismissing the cook who they complained cooked only typical Karnataka cuisine. His Kerala dishes tasted nothing like what we normally ate. I wondered what we were going to get tonight or if we might get anything palatable at all. My brother did cook once in a while but I wondered if they had ever cooked for more than five or six people at a time. Naveen may have but I wasn't so sure about Vishal. He was a foodie, but was he a good cook? I wasn't so sure.

Vishal came out from the kitchen just then and glared at me."You are going to eat your words very soon. Get ready to eat the yummiest biriyani in the whole wide world." It was then that he noticed Aathira. "Aha! So, is this your mystery girl from the hills?"

"Yes, Vishal. Aathira, meet Vishal, the second son of my maternal aunt. He is a paediatrician," I said making the introduction.

"Hi, Aathira. Nice to finally meet you. We all thought you existed only in Navneet's imagination. I hope you have met my wife Shalini and our little bundle of joy," said Vishal, as he sat next to Shalini.

"She came in just now. We were just getting to know her," said Shalini, smiling at Aathira.

"Where is Kishore? Is he in the kitchen too?" I asked. When I was going down to meet Aathira, he was right here in the living room talking to the others.

"He is in the media room, playing games with Aditya," said Shreya, coming out from the guest bedroom that was at the other end of the living room. Shreya came straight to Aathira and soon, they were all talking to each other. Arya was talking to Trisha and Riddhi and urging them to help themselves to the snacks laid out on the coffee table.

My eyes kept wandering to Aathira. Was she comfortable? She was smiling and answering the questions from the women around her but she kept twiddling her thumbs. I knew that she did that when she was agitated. Being surrounded by all these new people who she felt obliged to please wouldn't be easy for her. And more than anything else, I wanted her for myself. I was craving to kiss her again. She looked so delectable. I decided to intervene.

"Guys, let me steal my girl for a moment. You can talk to her after dinner. I haven't even shown her around the house," I said, and thankfully, none of them objected.

I held out my hand to Aathira. When she kept her hand in mine, I pulled her up and quickly put an arm around her waist. All the women around harrumphed loudly. I ignored them and guided her forward, deciding to start with the kitchen.

"The kitchen is out of limits as of now. I just came to kiss my little one," said Vishal. After planting a kiss on his sleeping baby, he mouthed 'enjoy' to me. He clearly understood me more than the others.

I loved my home and I couldn't wait to show it to Aathira. Initially, I bought it as an investment to sell it at a better rate. But after the interior designer had worked on it based on my ideas, it had become my favourite place in the world. I had everything I needed here, under one roof.

I led Aathira to the media room that was right next to the living room.

"You were just lucky. I gave in just because I was bored," Kishore was saying to Aditya as we walked in. His son had obviously beaten him again.

"It's time you accepted defeat gracefully," I told him.

"He never will," said Aditya, shaking his head.

Kishore rolled his eyes. "Ah, you must be Aathira," he said when he saw who I was with.

I quickly made the introductions.

"There are seven billion people out there in the world and you chose this crybaby?" he asked Aathira.

"Crybaby?" I protested.

"Of course. You used to cry at the drop of a hat back while you were in school, remember?" said Kishore, grinning widely. I wished I could punch him. He used to bully us all so much during our childhood, just because he was the oldest and the strongest.

"That was because you were such a big bad bully," I retorted.

"You know what, Aathira, he used to scream and cry buckets even if I just prodded him. I got scolded so many times because he is such a drama queen," said Kishore.

I wanted to kick him right where it would hurt the most. He was such a terror back then and my tears were my only weapon. Aathira looked amused.

"But I have to say this. No one is more loving than him in our entire family. No wonder he is Ammamma's pet," he continued and patted my shoulder.

I beamed at him. I forgave him instantly for revealing my childhood nickname to Aathira. Then, in another act of benevolence, he piled out of the room dragging Adithya with him who was about to start another game. He winked at me and clicked the door closed as he moved out. I locked it from the inside.

Aathira was standing in front of the LED screen that covered one wall and was inspecting the various settings.

I approached her, my heart thumping against my chest in anticipation. My body was screaming for her warmth.

The media room could seat around twenty people at a time and was designed as a centralized meeting area to watch sports, play games, and movies, or listen to music. Kishore hadn't switched off the player and I quickly scanned through the settings and selected the instrumental rendition of 'A *thousand years*' by Christina Perri.

As the song floated out, Aathira gazed at me. I quickly closed the distance between us, wound my arms around her waist and pulled her closer.

"Shall we dance?" I whispered, as I leaned closer and tipped up her chin.

"Yes," she said, as colour bloomed in her cheeks.

As we swayed to the music, I admired the woman in my arms. She was sparkling like sunlight on the ocean. She felt soft like snow but was warm as the summer. My earthly goddess. I loved her with all my heart and couldn't wait to make her mine. I enjoyed how gracefully she moved. I whirled her around and then pulled her closer to me so that her back was pressed to me. Her chest was rising and falling rapidly as she leaned on me. I trailed my hands up her arms in sync with the music and caressed her shoulders. From there, I dragged my palm down her chest, cupped her breasts and kneaded them, my thumbs flicking the beaded peaks through the many layers of her clothes. I heard her indrawn breath and I hardened painfully. She turned around swiftly, pressing her upturned face on my chest. She smelled like lavender and roses. Her eyes were dark with desire and her lips had parted slightly. She reached up and touched my face.

"I love ...," she began and then paused.

"You love what, darling?" I asked, pulling her tighter against me, desire roaring through me like a rapid in the hills.

"You... us... this moment," she whispered and I took her mouth in a hungry kiss. Her lips parted and my tongue slid right in. As always, I lost myself instantly in a whirlpool of sensuousness. As I deepened the kiss, I trailed my hand down and scrunched her dress up. A soft curse escaped my lips when instead of warm skin, my fingers encountered silk. I was craving to run my palms on her naked thighs, trail my finger between her legs and plunge my fingers into her warmth until she came apart in my arms.

A knock on the door broke the moment.

Aathira stepped away with a start and smoothed her clothes.

"Shall I open it?" she asked, moving towards the door.

"Wait. I need a minute," I said, willing my erection to go down.

Aathira looked at me and went all red when she understood what I meant.

I blew a breath and looked away. If I continued to look at her, the sucker between my legs wasn't going to calm down.

The knock this time was louder. I turned off the music and walked towards the door. I opened it a crack and peered out.

It was Kishore.

"There are other rooms in the house, you know!" he said, with a mischievous look in his eyes. I was going to kill this cock-blocker.

"Shut up and get lost," I snapped at him. He guffawed.

"Come on. They are about to serve dinner. They sent me to get you," he said and shrugged. As if he had nothing to do with the urgent dinner invitation.

I was a hundred per cent sure that he had come to just get a rise out of me. Once a bully, always a bully.

"Give me ten minutes. I have to show her around," I said, pushing him away.

Kishore shrugged again before he walked away.

Aathira was trying hard not to laugh when I turned to look at her.

"Shall we go? I heard there are other rooms in the house," she said grinning widely.

I punished her with a lingering kiss.

As I was revelling in the wonder that was her mouth, I heard someone clearing their throat loudly from outside. This time, it was Ananya. She gave me a sage smile and waved at Aathira.

"Are you guys so jobless?" I asked Ananya, much to the amusement of Aathira.

"Ammamma is waiting for you both to have dinner along with the rest of us," she said sweetly.

I sighed in exasperation.

"Come and check yourself if you doubt my words. Show her around after dinner. At this pace, you will take all night to finish the tour," she said, giving me a loaded look. She dusted her hands, kept them akimbo and stared at me as if she'd fight me if I didn't listen to her.

"Okay, okay, understood," I said but I wasn't ready to part with Aathira yet. With my crazy cousins around, I had known it would be hard to enjoy even a few minutes alone with Aathira.

"Come, Aathira. Ammamma wants to sit with you," Ananya said and tutted when I blocked her path.

The girls looked at each other and burst out laughing. Ananya walked out of the room the next minute, holding the hand of my girl, leaving me gawking at them.

When I walked into the dining room, I realized that Kishore and Ananya were speaking the truth. To my disappointment, Aathira was sitting next to Ammamma and Ananya was sitting on her other side. Ananya, that annoying chit, gave me a knowing smile when she saw me. The brat was doing this on purpose. I had all the mind to box her ears. I held myself back only because I knew their eyes were on me.

The only seat left was next to Arjun. I sat on the chair and glared at Ananya, who glared right back at me.

"Cheer up, pal. I know she took your place to irritate you. Let her enjoy her small victory. Anyway, I like your girl. You both make a fine pair," said Arjun, cheering me up.

I decided to forgive his brat of a wife just because she married this man who had become my closest friend and mentor over the years. Arjun helped me a lot when I was setting up my company. With his help, it had almost been a cakewalk. He was my first angel investor because he believed in my vision for the company. Even now, he was the one I approached when I had any tough business decisions to make. His expertise in managing his worldwide supermarket chain had given me the courage to expand QIS. Now, I had branches in Mumbai, Delhi and Dubai though they weren't as fully-fledged as the Bengaluru one. We were also contemplating opening one in Seoul early next year. Rohit was still hesitating, but I knew he wanted it too. After all, he had roots there.

I looked at Aathira. She looked happy surrounded by my dear ones. Her friends too looked like they were enjoying the evening. And to my surprise, the food tasted really good.

"Wow, guys! I didn't know you could cook such yummy biriyani. This is good," I said, giving them a thumbs up.

"Why are you so surprised? After all these years, you still don't know that I am India's answer to Gordon Ramsey?" asked Vishal, and Shalini snickered loudly.

"Oh, is that why you flipped out when I suggested we use frozen chicken?" asked Naveen.

"Yeah, bro! Like Gordon Ramsey says, 'Fresh ingredients are the only way to guarantee a great taste.' See, the biriyani tastes amazing because I went out and brought fresh chicken," replied Vishal.

"All Vishal did was bring the ingredients. Poor Naveen did everything else. See how shamelessly he is hogging the limelight. Gordon Ramsey, huh?" Arjun whispered to me and we snorted.

"Nay. It tastes amazing because I added that extra pinch of salt and pepper. You idiots had almost ruined it," interjected Kishore, who was sitting next to Naveen.

Naveen raised his eyes heavenward but didn't say anything.

"Come on, don't take credit for Naveen's hard work so shamelessly. I was watching you both," said Shreya, looking at Kishore and Vishal.

"Yeah, Vishal kept leaving the kitchen every five minutes citing one excuse or another," said Shalini, teaming up with Shreya to roast their husbands. Arya was trying hard not to join in.

"Aathira, didn't you see? I was there in the kitchen the whole time. Shalini, you traitor. Et Tu, Brute?!" whined Vishal dramatically.

"Enough, kids. I know exactly who did what as well. So stop fighting and let's eat," said Ammamma putting a temporary stop to all the ruckus going around.

I looked around the table. The only people missing were my mother and aunts who had decided to visit Ananya's home in Bangalore at her mother's request. Tomorrow the team, the entire Sreepuram gang, was going there. From there, they would part and this magnificent month of us being together would come to an end.

At the beginning of our joint vacation, I hadn't thought even in my wildest dreams that I'd find my soulmate by the time it ended. If my mother knew Aathira was here tonight, she would have dashed here to meet the girl who had finally won her son's heart. But as it was a last-minute decision to bring Aathira home, I hadn't told her.

Aathira looked up just then and our eyes met. My whole body heated up and all the voices around us vanished. In the short time I had been with her, I'd felt so inexplicably happy and fulfilled than I ever had.

I couldn't wait to have her alone with me again. And from the way her eyes glittered, I knew she was hoping for that too.

20

Aathira

The grand old matriarch with her boisterous, nettling gang of grandkids and great-grandkids won my heart in no time. Within a few minutes of me joining them, they were dragging me into their banters and silly fights. I was literally playing referee most of the time.

My very own dog whisperer, her pet grandkid, kept trying to drag me away from them so that he could have his way with me. His attempts were continuously thwarted by his gang of brothers and their spouses. They found inventive ways to come between us.

One or the other person was always with us, with the result that we did not get even a single moment alone after the few minutes of bliss we shared in the media room.

Shreya, Navneet's eldest cousin Kishore's wife, rescued me from the chaos while Navneet was busy fighting off his cousins over some new ruckus they had created.

"Come let us walk around. I will show you the house. When they are together, the cousins can be worse than middle schoolers. You should see how they fight over food. These grown men act like toddlers. They were initially planning to make *pradhaman* for dessert and I had to veto it. If not, they would mash bananas into the *payasam* and have eating competitions. And after that, they would have collapsed on the couches with their swollen bellies and snored away. They do it every single time," Shreya told me as we reached the upper floor of the penthouse.

Shreya showed me Navneet's well-equipped home office which had a separate entrance from the top floor. Apart from the three bedrooms on the bottom floor, the top floor of the penthouse housed the master bedroom along with another smaller bedroom. Every nook and corner of the apartment looked like it had received special attention from the designer. Though every room was spacious, the spaces were utilized well and were a sight to behold. They must be employing an army of maids to upkeep this house. Just as we were entering the master bedroom, Navneet dashed upstairs.

"Ah, Shreya, here you are. Your son is looking for you. Go," said Navneet. It was clearly a lie. Shreya had tucked Aditya to bed before accompanying me. She raised two perfectly shaped eyebrows at Navneet.

"Please, go. And stop those idiots from marching up here. I will take you around Chikpet market to hunt for the fabrics you were talking about. I promise," said Navneet.

Shreya, I was told, was an established fashion designer and ran a popular boutique in Dubai. Navneet's bribe did not work obviously because Shreya just stood in the room scratching her cheek.

"See...," Shreya began.

Navneet looked pissed now. He looked at me and then glared at Shreya.

"For God's sake, I haven't had a peaceful moment with my girl without one of you barging in every time. Go, Shreya. I promise. I will take you around Chikpet tomorrow morning itself."

"Promise?" Shreya asked.

"Promise," repeated Navneet.

Shreya leaned closer and stage whispered in my ears, "In case he tries some hanky-panky, just holler, okay? I will keep my ears wide open."

Navneet heard it and grunted like a bull.

I couldn't help but snicker.

Once Shreya was out of the room, Navneet wound his arms around me and held me close.

"Did my mad family annoy you a lot?" he asked. He frowned as he searched my face. Did he really think I was getting upset by the antics of his cousins?

"No way. They were very nice to me. I like them," I told him.

"Thank God. Because even though I love them to bits, there are moments when I wish to throw a nuclear bomb at them. Trust me, you can't find a bigger gang of such coordinated bullies anywhere else. If I am not wrong, at this very moment, Shreya is instigating them to come up here. And this will continue till we get married."

My jaw dropped open. Till we get married? When did I agree to marry him?

"Excuse me! Who said I was marrying you?" I asked, pumped by the bully energy I had imbibed from his cousins.

"You too?! Come on. That is the proper way ahead for us," he said.

"I don't even know you properly. I didn't know you were this filthy rich. What if all these promises you are making are just to get into my pants? Oh, I have read tons of romances where the billionaire dumps girls once he gets what he wants," I said just to rile him. But the poor guy blanched.

"No, Aathira. I have never felt this way about another girl. I have never brought a girl home to meet my family. Only you. Don't you see that?" Navneet reasoned.

I didn't have the heart to tease him anymore. I smiled at him.

"Dumbo. I was just teasing you. But I need a proper proposal if I have to agree to marry you," I said. I stood on my toes and planted a kiss on his cheeks.

He smiled at me. He cupped my cheeks and kissed me on my mouth. After a lingering kiss, he stepped away. Placing his hands on my shoulders, he turned me around to face the master bedroom.

"How do you like our room?"

Our room! I liked the sound of it.

The room looked like a dream. It was wide enough to fit Riddhi's entire flat into it and was designed in the same colour scheme as the living room. White and gold. An exquisite marble mosaic painting of an entwined couple faced the four-poster bed which stood at the centre of the room. The wall facing one side of the bed was completely made of floor-to-roof panelled glass, giving a magnificent glimpse of the shining city of Bangalore and the night sky.

"I dreamed about us here, today morning you know. You in my arms, our limbs intertwined, just like that couple in the painting and me making sweet love to you," he said, pulling me closer and hugging me from behind.

Nuzzling my hair, he whispered, "Do you dream about me?"

I almost shook my head. Why was I lying? I nodded. My dreams were becoming more and more explicit with each passing day and I would wake up all hot and bothered.

Navneet ran his tongue along my earlobe and I trembled in his arms. He pushed my hair away from my left shoulder and kissed the crook of my neck. He trailed kisses all over my shoulder and then he pushed the sleeves of my dress to kiss the top of my cleavage. Darts of pleasure hit my core and I wound my hand around his neck, pressing my lips to his. He captured my lower lip between his teeth and nibbled them. It felt so good. So good that my legs felt like jelly and I sagged against him even as little mewling sounds escaped me. I could feel his hardness press against my stomach. Proof that he desired me as much as I wanted him.

"Where did you say he was?" Kishore's voice reached us from the stairwell just before we heard footsteps. Multiple. It seemed like Kishore was not alone.

"The weasels," cursed Navneet. He guided me out of the room and down a corridor that led to a staircase.

"I know the perfect place to hide," said Navneet as he led me up the narrow stairs. The stairs ended on the terrace. The sudden rush of cold, night breeze assaulted my senses. But the scene in front made me catch my breath.

Bathed in the moonlight was a beautiful terrace garden, complete with a garden swing and a couple of lawn chairs around a tea table. The scent of night blossoms filled the air. At the other end of the garden, glittering like a blue gem in the moonlight was a wide pool.

"Lovely," I exclaimed.

"I hope to spend many evenings with you here very soon," said Navneet. "But right now, we need to hide."

He guided me to a corner of the garden where two big, wide columns held a small tank of some sort on top of them.

"Don't make a sound. If we even breathe a little loudly, they will find us," he warned me.

Soon his bro-gang arrived and began looking around.

"I don't think he would have come here. He might have gone out through the home office door. At this moment, he most probably would be at a café' with Aathira. Okay, let's go now," said Kishore, as he looked around.

"We tortured him enough anyway. Let's not scare his girl away. Then he will start moaning and whining the way he did last week," agreed Naveen.

"I should just kill them," Navneet muttered beside me.

I struggled to keep a chuckle from escaping from my mouth.

Once his bullies left, we got out from the shadows of the columns. To my surprise, on the other side of the garden was an indoor volleyball court. Navneet showed me around and then we returned to the garden.

He made me sit on the garden swing and then lay on it keeping his head on my lap.

"Can you swim?" he asked.

"Of course. I am a girl from the hills, remember? What do you expect? I learned to swim from a wild stream that passes through the jungle. The water would be ice cold in the mornings, so Appa used to take me swimming in the afternoons. The only problem was during the monsoons when the place would be crawling with leeches," I told him.

"We have a village pond next to Ammamma's home. As children, swimming was one of our favourite pastimes during our summer vacations there. When I saw this property with a private swimming pool, I bought it immediately. At first, I had bought it as an investment. But now it has become home."

"Who all live here with you?" I asked.

"Only Naveen and Arya as of now. Their villa will be ready to move in by the end of the next month and then I will be all alone. But I don't plan to be alone for long. You will come home, right?" he asked.

I hesitated because everything still felt like a dream. I feared my alarm might ring the next moment ending this very vivid dream. When I did not answer, Navneet wound his arm around my head and made me look at his face.

"Aathira, will you come home by then?" he asked again.

"I would love to. But I haven't met your parents. Will they like me?"

"You don't need any more approval. You have met most of my family. My father is no more. Naveen is the fatherly figure in my family. My mother already liked you when I showed her your picture."

"My picture. Where did you get my picture? Your friend, your cousins... everyone says I look prettier than my picture. Tell me, where did they see my picture?"

"I flicked it from our college's Facebook page. Do you remember that picture of you dancing at the dance festival? You are wearing a similar dress in that photo," he confessed with a goofy smile.

"This is the same dress. It is a gift from my friends. Ah, so why! You are such a pathetic stalker."

"You have no idea how pathetic I was. Wait. Let me show you the moment I fell in love with you," he said and after scrolling through his phone for a while, he showed me a pic.

It was of me dancing around the fire wearing my white polka dot dress.

"How?" I asked searching his face. "Is there something else about that night I don't know? Did you know me before that?"

"No. I met you for the first time that day. And at first sight, I fell hard and how! Trust me, for a moment I thought you were the creation of my agitated mind. An illusion. You looked like a pagan Goddess who was going to shoo away all my troubles. I took this photo to convince myself you were human," he said with a wide smile.

I traced his lips with my thumb and then bent down to kiss him. As he devoured my lips, I wondered how I had gotten this lucky. On the saddest day of my life, this man walked into my world and made it bloom like a mountain in springtime. He was a storm and I was the fallen leaf. He held me in his bosom and blew life back into me.

Just then, Navneet got a call. He ignored it the first time, but when his phone rang the second time, he blew out a breath and picked it up.

"What is it now, Naveen?" he asked, picking up the phone.

He listened to Naveen's words and he stood up, his face red with anger.

"Enough with your pranks. I've had enough of this," Navneet snapped at him.

But whatever Naveen said after that, made his eyes go wide and he staggered. He held onto me for support, and I knew for sure that something terrible had happened.

"It is Ammamma. She just collapsed. We have to hurry," said Navneet, his breath now rapid and his face pale.

I hugged him tight as he leaned against me and burst into sobs.

"She will be alright. Don't worry, okay? Nothing will happen to her," I said, as Navneet dragged himself up. His chest was heaving with stifled sobs. I knew how much he loved his Ammamma. She was like the heart centre of this family. If something happened to her, they wouldn't be able to bear it.

I said a quick prayer for her wellness mentally and rushed down into the house with Navneet.

21

Navneet

Aathira patted my hand as we waited inside the private room we had booked for Ammamma. I was grateful that she was with me. I felt stronger with Aathira beside me. All the way to the hospital, she kept telling me to not worry and that everything was going to be fine. Though I'd told her initially that she could return to her apartment with her friends, she insisted on accompanying me. In the short time that Aathira had known her, she had come to care for Ammamma.

Ammamma was stable as of now according to the doctors though she hadn't regained consciousness yet. None of us knew what exactly was wrong with her. She had simply collapsed while on her way to her room to retire for the night. Vishal and Arjun had rushed her to this super speciality hospital that was a good half an hour farther from our place, even though we had a good hospital just near our apartment complex.

Did Ammamma have any health issues that we were not aware of? Vishal and Arjun were her official in-house doctors and she would consult no one else for her health issues. Whatever it was, it looked like Vishal and Arjun had kept us in the dark.

Once Ammamma's condition was pronounced stable, Vishal and Arjun met with one of the specialists here who happened to be their senior in college. When they returned, they looked morose.

"What is it? What happened to her?" asked Ananya, voicing the question every one of us was waiting to ask.

Vishal cleared his throat and addressed us.

"I've kept a secret from you all at Ammamma's request. Five months ago, I ran a liver function test on Ammamma because of some vague symptoms I noticed in her. She was diagnosed with an advanced stage of liver cirrhosis. The doctors gave her a maximum of nine months to live. It was the reason why she wanted all of us to spend this past month with her," said Vishal, before he paused unable to carry on.

"But how? She looks so healthy. She is the most health-conscious person in the family. She went for regular checkups. You know that," said Naveen.

"Chronic liver disease can be a silent killer. It sometimes stays undiagnosed till it progresses to a deadly stage. In fact, she did not show any serious symptoms. I suspected it only when her blood tests threw up some unexpected results," explained Vishal.

I blew out a breath to calm my racing heart.

"So was this past month her way of bidding goodbye to us?" asked Shreya, her eyes brimming with tears.

Vishal nodded.

"She wasn't ready to go for a liver transplant operation which is the only viable option for her to survive this," said Vishal.

"You should have told us. We could have tried to convince her," said Kishore. "She cannot leave us so soon.

Not after the memories we've just made together. I was even thinking we should make this kind of a get-together an annual event."

"Trust me, I tried. But you know how stubborn she can be. But I have been consulting with my senior who works here since then. He had asked me to bring her here. I even made an appointment for the day after tomorrow. But then tonight this happened..."

"What can be done now? What did your senior say? Let's not leave any leaf unturned to help her," I said, and the others immediately agreed with me.

"As I said before, a liver transplant is the only solution. And it has to be done quickly. Time is running out for her," said Vishal.

"Let's go ahead with that then. Ammamma might be ready to leave us, but I am not ready to let her go yet. I am sure none of us is," I said. My heart clenched painfully just at the thought of living in a world without Ammamma. I'd donate my liver to her in the blink of an eye. Maybe she knew what we would do and that was why she had refused to undergo a transplant.

"In India, a live donor can only be a relative, spouse or friend who is between the age of nineteen and sixty. That was the reason she was against it. She didn't want any of us to go through the trauma of such a major surgery for her sake," said Vishal, confirming my suspicions.

"If I am not wrong, there is no permanent damage to the donor, right? I remember a colleague in my former company who had donated his liver to his mother. He was back at work in two months," I said.

"Yes. True. But there can be unseen complications as it is major surgery for both the donor as well as the recipient," chipped in Arjun.

"Whatever. I want Ammamma to undergo the surgery. When she regains consciousness, I am going to convince her," said Ananya.

Vishal and Arjun exchanged a look on hearing Ananya's words. Then Vishal turned to us.

"Chances of her regaining consciousness enough to make such a decision are very low according to the doctors. Unless we take the decision and make her undergo the surgery, our dear Ammamma won't return. She will spend the rest of her days in bed, connected to various life support systems," he said.

Silence spread through the room like doom. Ananya was the first to burst into sobs. Shalini followed and soon every single eye in the room was teary. My heart felt like it would burst from the sadness burgeoning inside me. Kishore walked away to the window and was holding onto the frame, as he shook with sobs. Naveen sagged onto the door looking visibly shaken and Aathira was trying to console Arya who was sobbing like a child. Vishal and Arjun were holding each other's hands, trying to be each other's strength.

Just then a knock sounded. Naveen opened the door. My aunts and my mother dashed into the room.

"What happened to Amma? She was fine when we left yesterday. What happened?" cried Uma Aunty as she shook Vishal.

It took a while to calm them down and get them to understand what had happened. When they heard everything from Vishal, their wails grew louder. My mom looked like she would collapse at any moment. Arya held her and she sobbed hugging her.

"I am ready to be the donor. Let's go and do the necessary tests," I said because I knew every ticking second that we were wasting by crying over what had already happened was going to delay us from taking the necessary steps to prevent her from dying. We needed Ammamma to return to us healthy and hearty.

"Me too," said Naveen. Almost everyone in the room immediately expressed their desire to be her liver donor.

"Okay, listen. That is good. We will ask the hospital to test all of us. I am sure one of us will be able to help her," said Arjun.

"Yes. We were discussing just that with the specialists here. We need to find someone compatible with Ammamma's blood type. Along with that, the donor should be in good physical and mental health too," explained Vishal.

With the decisions thus made, some semblance of peace returned to the room. Vishal explained to us that his senior, Dr Rajendra Bhatt, had already performed hundreds of such transplant surgeries and he was confident of bringing Ammamma back if we could find a donor at the earliest.

From what Vishal explained to us, the evaluation tests for the donors would take a minimum of two weeks. Blood tests, chest X-ray, CT scan, electrocardiogram (EKG), physical exam and tissue matching were some of the tests we would undergo.

Shalini, my mother and my aunts were taken off of the donor's list because they didn't meet the criteria. Shalini was dissuaded from being a donor as she was a new mother. My aunts and mom were also ruled out by Arjun and Vishal because of their lifestyle illnesses.

The rest of us filled out forms to register ourselves as potential liver donors for Ammamma.

Now, the only thing we could do was to wait.

22

Aathira

It had been a blessing. There wasn't another word that could justify the moments I experienced after entering Navneet's house. The bubble of joy we were in, however, had shattered when Navneet's grandmother collapsed.

Even now, as I looked around, I felt admiration for each member of the Sreepuram family. Each one was grieving yet they were trying to act bravely to become each other's strength. After Navneet and the others had filled the form for the tests, he took me to his mother, made me sit near her and left without another word.

Navneet's mother turned to me with her eyes brimming with tears. She tried to smile at me and failed. She grabbed my left hand and squeezed it.

"I am so sorry that we are meeting at such a time. We were all eagerly waiting to meet you ever since Navneet told us about you. I have so many things to tell you, but, right now my words fail me," she said and choked on her last word.

"Please don't apologize. I understand. But this will pass. Ammamma will be back and healthy very soon," I said trying to reassure her.

"Be with Navneet, okay? He is trying to act brave but Amma is his weakness. He dotes on her. Cheer him up, won't you?" Her sad eyes implored me.

"I will," I said, squeezing her hand.

It should have felt awkward sitting with Navneet's mother like this. But it didn't. She felt like a grieving relative who needed my support.

Navneet's aunts joined us and made small talk with me. Each member I talked with, was doing their best to make me feel at ease, even though they were struggling with their own inner turmoil. There was no hostility in any of their interactions. All their energies were focused on the one person who was fighting for her life inside the ICU.

Their worried faces loomed inside my mind as Navneet drove me back to my accommodation.

"Let me know how I can help you or anyone in any way, okay?" I said to him when he stopped the car in the basement parking.

"Just be my strength, Aathira. Whenever my worries overwhelm me, I think about you. Joy and hope then find their way back to me. You are my blessing. I don't know how I would have dealt with everything without you today," he said, and I kissed his cheeks.

He pulled me into his arms and gave me a gentle, lingering kiss. It was not a lust-filled kiss, but one packed with love. He seemed to draw energy from it, and so did I.

"I want Ammamma with me when I marry you. I want her to hold our kids and make them laugh. She will do all that, right, sweetheart?" asked Navneet. His eyes were misty. My own filled with tears.

To be his lover itself was a dream come true. To be his wife seemed like a distant possibility. Yet, Navneet was talking about it as if it was something that was surely going to happen. I wanted his wishes to come true, as mine were no different. Who wouldn't wish their kids to have a great-grandmother like Arundhati Mukundan? Only a privileged few were blessed that way.

"Of course. She will be there to bless us in every happy moment," I said hoping with all my heart that my words would come true.

We walked hand in hand to my flat and then he returned to the hospital.

Riddhi and Trisha hadn't slept and were deep in discussion when I entered the flat.

"Is she alright?" they asked together, the second I sat on the couch.

When I told them everything I had learnt at the hospital about her condition, their faces fell.

"I just love that woman. I was praying that she would be alright. You should have seen the way Navneet's cousins screamed when she collapsed. There was not a single dry eye in the room. It is proof of how much they love her," said Riddhi.

"Yes. My grandmother was a terror and absolutely no one loved her toward the end of her life. Arundhati Aunty is so loving. She made sure we were at ease today even though we are nobodies, as far as she is concerned," said Trisha, as she sat up on the couch hugging a cushion.

"Yeah. Navneet was telling me that his grandmother becomes a godmother to almost everyone she meets. Irrespective of gender, age or social status, she treats everyone the same way and showers them with love. It is really a privilege that we got to meet her," I said remembering Navneet's words about his grandmother.

"Yes. Absolutely. Just message in the group also. Sneha might be anxiously waiting to hear what happened. We already talked on a video call once with her to tell her everything. She must be expecting an update from you," said Riddhi.

"I will message her."

I messaged Sneha and I realized she was still awake. She called me immediately and conveyed her wishes and prayers for Arundhati Mukundan.

"Don't worry. With so many of us praying for her welfare, God will make sure she is hale and hearty soon. You need to cheer Navneet up. More positivity is the need of the hour," she said before hanging up.

Once I showered and changed into my nightdress, I called Navneet and spoke to him for a few minutes. He wished me a good night before hanging up and promised to keep me updated on his grandmother's condition.

Then I peeped into the living room where the two were still watching some movie on Netflix.

"Girls, go to sleep. And please wake me up on time in case I don't. Trisha, remember, tomorrow we are learning some key concepts in our training. Navneet has asked us not to miss day two of the training," I said. He had insisted I go to work when I told him that I could take the day off to be with him and his family.

"Oh, I see," said Riddhi and I saw her exchanging glances with Trisha. They were back in teasing mode.

I withdrew to my room as I wasn't in the mood for it. I knew they were bursting to grill me about what had happened between Navneet and me while I was alone with him at his home.

Just the memory of me in his arms erased most of the alarming thoughts reverberating inside my head and I fell asleep almost as soon as my head hit the pillow.

23

Navneet

I remember watching a 'shot of awe' video by Jason Silva on YouTube where he talked about the three kinds of deaths according to the Mexicans. The first death occurred when we became aware of our mortality. That first moment when we realized we would all die one day. The second death was when we actually died, when our body no longer functioned on its own, and was returned to earth. The third and the most definitive death, was when there was no one left alive to remember us. I had played it on loop the first time because the man had a way with his words. The message was disheartening in a way yet it was imprinted indelibly in my memory.

Now with the possibility of death lurking near a dear one, I was thinking constantly of death and mortality. Ammamma was a loving soul who had touched the lives of so many people through her words and her kindness. Many would remember her gratefully even after she was gone. Her creations, her books would continue to win over people's hearts even when her heart ceased functioning. Her legacy would live on, defying death.

According to her, death was the only thing that was certain in this world. Life was uncertain. No one entered this world with a permanent visa. We all eventually died. What mattered was how we chose to fill the moments between our birth and death, and what difference we brought into the life of the people around us.

But none of us was ready to allow her to embrace the second death. So, even as she drifted in and out of consciousness inside the ICU, we ran around to bring her back to our world.

So it was utter relief when I learned that I was a perfect match to be a living liver donor for Ammamma. I could bring her back. Even amid that happiness, I could sense a dread within the Sreepuram family. Maybe it was natural. At the same time, the two of us would be undergoing a major operation. I could understand their angst.

As the first step, I was briefed by the surgeon in charge, Dr Rajendra Bhatt. His team of doctors were with him. I was accompanied by Arjun and Vishal who asked the appropriate questions. I just listened as they discussed in detail every aspect of the surgery, the recovery phase and also what precautions had to be taken.

Once they were done, the doctor dismissed them, wanting to speak privately with me.

"As you may have heard, we are going to do a less invasive surgery on you which will shorten your recovery period. So, you needn't worry at all. Within two weeks, you will feel almost back to normal. But yes, the liver takes up to 6 to 8 weeks to regenerate itself to its original size, so you will have to take adequate precautions. I know you are a busy man, so I promise, you will be able to return to work within no time," said Dr Bhatt.

"I am not worried about myself. I have complete faith in you. I want you to promise that our grandmother will return to us hearty and healthy. I have no other requests."

"I will try my best."Dr Bhatt smiled at me as we shook hands.

As soon as I left the hospital, I texted Aathira.

Me: Come to my office. I have something important to tell you.

Her reply came the next minute.

Aathira: Oh no. We can't meet there. This girl will not keep her mouth shut. And everyone will know soon that we are lovers.

Me: Who cares? I want everyone to know that you are my girl. Nay, you are my queen.

Aathira: Dear king, your queen objects. The news of an office romance between the big boss and a new trainee will spread like wildfire in the company. Let's meet somewhere outside and away from the company.

Me: Okay, your wish is my command, my queen. Let's meet at the coffee shop near the apartment at 6 in the evening today.

But because of a meeting that ended late, by the time I met her, I had kept her waiting for over an hour. Trisha was with her and they both looked equally exasperated.

"Good that you came now. I might have committed murder if you were late by another minute," said Aathira, when I walked up to their table.

"Sorry. An urgent meeting delayed me," I apologised as I sat on the empty chair next to her.

"Hey, it is okay. I am not angry at you," Aathira said.

"You're not? Why are you in a murderous mood then? What happened?" I asked.

Aathira rolled her eyes and didn't say a thing. I raised my eyebrow and looked at Trisha. She just shrugged in answer. What was going on?

"She is practising speaking in Korean and is forcing me to become her conversation partner. She wasn't uttering a word in any other language. Imagine!" said Aathira.

I couldn't help but smile. Aathira had told me all about Trisha's love for everything Korean.

"She isn't helping at all. I have taken up this 90-day challenge to become fluent in Korean. And this is part of the challenge," said Trisha.

"Korean sounds like Greek to me, okay? Stop making me read all these practice sentences from the course you are taking. My head is spinning," complained Aathira.

"Learn Korean. If not, how will you speak to my Oppa?" said Trisha, batting her eyelashes at Aathira.

Aathira looked at me, her eyes pleading for help.

Trisha looked at me and smiled beatifically.

"If you will promise to send me to Korea when you open a QIS branch there, I will spare your girlfriend and leave you two alone. Else, I do like being the third wheel, you know!" said Trisha, batting her eyelashes at me now.

Aathira hissed out a breath and narrowed her eyes at Trisha.

"If you become fluent in Korean, do we have any other choice?" I asked, wondering how she had heard about our plans to expand to Korea. The plans for the Korean branch were still in a nascent stage and almost wholly depended on Rohit.

"I know, you are the best. I will leave you then in the pleasant company of your beautiful girlfriend. Aathira, don't forget. The curfew starts at ten. No entry after that," said Trisha, and then whispered something in her friend's ears and took off before Aathira could respond. Aathira went all red.

"Ignore if you heard anything," she said, continuing to blush furiously.

What had Trisha said to make her blush that way? I really wanted to know.

Aathira fidgeted with her purse and then softly asked, "How is Ammamma? Did she get a donor?"

"Yes. That is what I came to tell you," I said. Even before I said anything, Aathira blanched.

"It's you, right?" she asked, her eyes wide and wary.

"Yes. We got the results today and I am a perfect match. Isn't that great?" I said and Aathira grabbed my hand.

Her hands had gone cold. She looked petrified.

"Hey, don't worry. Nothing will happen, okay? The doctors are highly skilled," I said, covering her hand with mine.

"Of course. But...," she said and I could see that her eyes were filled with tears.

Ignoring the fact that we were in a public place, I gathered her in my arms and kissed the top of her head. I could feel her trembling with silent sobs.

"Okay. I have looked up the operation in detail and the doctors briefed me also. I am not going to look like a patched-up doll after the operation. My scars will also be minimal as they are doing a less invasive procedure," I said.

At that her sobs became audible. She punched my chest.

"As if the scars matter," she muttered between sobs.

I continued to hold her, trying to calm her down. Somehow, it felt good that she was shedding hot tears because she was worried about me. I squeezed her tightly and she pushed away from me and quietly dried her eyes with a tissue.

She didn't speak or look at me for the several long minutes that followed. Her deep inhales and exhales were the only sounds I could hear.

"I will take you with me the next time I visit the doctor. You can speak to him. Maybe then your worries will cease?" I said.

"My father was in an accident a few years ago and he had to undergo an operation to replace his injured femur bone. He had this dazed look on his face even after he was brought out of the operation theatre because of the effect of anaesthetics. At that moment, I thought he would never speak to or recognize me ever again. I remember the pain he experienced during the recovery period and all the struggles to get back up on his leg. This is going to be an even more complex operation. To be honest, Navneet, I am terrified. I don't think I can bear to see you in pain."

I could understand her. I was apprehensive too, but it was the bigger picture that kept me calm.

"I am ready to bear any pain if it can save Ammamma. And I am sure, God will keep me safe."

"Of course. I'm sorry for being so selfish. I wasn't thinking clearly. Please forgive me," she said, looking away.

"Aathira, please don't apologize. I am honestly happy that you are worried. It means a lot to hear that you can't bear to see me in pain. It means a lot that you care so much. I don't want any other reaction from you. I want you to be selfish when it comes to me. And trust me, I am extremely selfish when it comes to you," I told her, slipping my hands around her waist and pulling her closer to me. We sat that way till the waiter came to take our order.

It took a while for Aathira to calm down but by the time we left the cafeteria, she was smiling again. In the deserted basement parking of her apartment, I switched off the car engine and in the darkened car, pulled her into my arms. I kissed her then, relishing the feel of her warm mouth and soft body against me. I would've done so much more if another car hadn't pulled up just then. I had to be content with holding her hand as we walked to her flat before returning to my empty bed at home.

I couldn't wait to hold her close and go to sleep. Sleep wouldn't be in question if she was with me on my bed though, would it? No way. I would undress her slowly, worship her body till she shivered in my arms and make love to her all night.

My imagination began to run wild and my body hardened making it necessary to go for a quick swim in the pool to cool down. Even there, I craved her. I could picture her there in the pool beside me and I began to fantasize about how she would look in a swimsuit and how it would feel to embrace her wet body. Defeated, I gave up and returned to my room. I spent the next few hours twitching on my bed trying to fall asleep.

The following days flew off in a blink as I had a lot of work-related stuff to settle before the operation. Most of my time was spent reassigning my duties. I signed a Power of Attorney to Rohit to ensure that none of the company operations suffered in my absence.

No one in the company except Rohit was aware that I would be undergoing an emergency operation. On paper, I was going away on a business trip to Dubai and all the company operations were to be managed by Rohit in the meanwhile.

"I am in awe of you, man. You are doing such a great thing. I don't know if I can ever do such a thing," said Rohit as we sat talking that weekend.

"I am grateful that I am getting a chance to do something for Ammamma. All her life, she helped others live better lives. I hope I can help her continue to do that for a lot more years."

"She sure will. I read that 53% of liver transplant recipients live for more than 20 years after the operation. I wish her even more."

"Thanks. Now that I have nothing scheduled, I feel free. Time to call my darling, I guess," I said, pulling out my phone to call Aathira.

In the rush to sort out my work commitments, and transfer my duties to Rohit, I could not make the time to spend any quality time with Aathira. Most of our interactions were over the phone. All my intentions to court her elaborately when I was free hence went for a toss. Yet, my girl wasn't complaining. In fact, every day the minutes I spent talking with her had become my salvation. She had been to the hospital to visit Ammamma multiple times along with Trisha and it seemed like my family members were seeing her more than me. I envied them but was relieved that they all seemed to dote on her.

I was to get admitted to the hospital on Sunday evening to prepare for the operation. The operation was scheduled for Wednesday morning. So, I decided to have a day-long date with Aathira because I knew it would be weeks before I'd be able to go on a proper date with her.

So, I made elaborate plans. I wanted her to remember our first real date forever.

24
Aathira

Have you ever had nagging anxiety even though everything seemed fine? When you become plagued by intrusive thoughts that start harmless but you become fixated on them till they become terrifying?

I was in such a phase even though I knew I had to get over my fears and not become Navneet's source of worry. Though I acted bravely on the outside, I was frantic inside. And I knew he could sense it. It would have all gone away if I could spend more time with him. But I had hardly seen him in the past few days. We did spend a lot of time talking over the phone though. I tried to not project my anxieties on him because I knew he needed to be stress-free.

My girls' gang was sending me articles to read to ward off my anxiety. Riddhi made enquiries about the doctor in charge and told me his success rate was super high. Trisha and Sneha tried to drag me into other trivial stuff to distract me. But nothing helped.

All I wanted was to be with Navneet but he wasn't even calling me that often. Usually, he called me at nine when he was having his dinner. Today he hadn't. I retired to my room with a new novel, refusing to watch a movie with the girls. My worry peaked around ten. I picked up my phone to call him when it rang. It was Navneet.

"Hi, love," he said in his deep, sexy voice and I heaved a sigh of relief. All my lingering anxieties melted away.

"I was just about to call you. Is everything okay?" I asked, sitting up on my bed, hugging a pillow.

"Everything is fine. Listen, I want to spend the whole day tomorrow with you. Can we?" he asked.

"Of course. I would love to," I said, my heart skipping at the happy thought.

"So, I have two plans. One is to take you around Bengaluru and the other to spend time with you at home, just you and me. What would you like? Before you choose, let me tell you, I prefer the latter," he said and I could sense him smiling at the other end of the line.

Of course, I wanted the latter too. I was sure roaming with him would be a pleasure. But he needed to relax before the operation. And as of now, I craved his company more.

"All I want is to be with you. Away from the eyes of everyone. Just you and me," I said.

"We are in luck then. Half of the Sreepuram gang has gone to Ananya's house. Arya and my brother have gone to some temple in North Karnataka along with my mother to pray for Ammamma and me. They will return only the day after tomorrow. But think clearly. We will be all alone. You are okay with that, right?"

"I am," I said, fully comprehending the implications of his statement. But nothing mattered other than being near him.

With the operation scheduled for Wednesday, every single moment in his company was precious. It would take weeks for him to recover once the transplant was done.

We decided to meet at a popular cafe adjacent to our apartment for breakfast and then from there, he'd take me to his home.

So, I left my flat at eight the next morning much to the amusement of Trisha and Riddhi. I turned a deaf year to their many innuendos. In my hurry to be with Navneet, I hadn't even taken the time to dress properly. I had pulled out a pair of jeans and a yellow *kurti* from my cupboard after a bath and was ready within ten minutes.

Navneet was waiting for me at the café. We had *podi idlis* (idlis coated with flavoursome chutney powder) that had lately become my favourite. A filter coffee followed and we were ready for a happy Sunday.

Navneet punched in the code to his home and after opening the door wide, he picked me up in his arms as if I weighed nothing.

"Welcome home, sweetheart," he said as he stepped inside carrying me. I wound my arms around his neck and gave him a peck on his cheek.

He smiled but didn't kiss me as I was expecting him to do. He put me down on one of the couches in the living room and then peppered my face with kisses. I giggled.

"Before I forget and get lost in your eyes, let me do the proper thing first. I have something for you," he said and opened a drawer under the coffee table. He took out a small jewellery box, opened it and pushed it towards me. Sitting pretty inside the velvet box were two beautiful platinum rings. Before I could truly take in what this meant, he picked the smaller one, held my left hand and quietly slid it on my finger.

"With this ring, I promise to be near you, to love you and care for you throughout my life," he declared, as he kissed my knuckles.

I didn't know how to respond. I gazed at him with my heart in my mouth.

"Now your turn," he said, pointing to the other ring in the box.

As my heart sang, I made him wear his ring and whispered, "I promise to love you and only you for all my entire life."

His eyes twinkled. He leaned near and dragged me onto his lap. His mouth devoured mine and he claimed me in every sense. It was as if nothing else remained in the world except what he was making me feel. Not even a thought. As we melted into each other, I felt his erection grow harder against me and my core clenched.

"Aathira..." he murmured, as he pulled me flush against his hard chest and kissed me over and over again. "I have been aching for you since the day I met you."

I sank into him deciding to let things take their course. I wanted this. Every atom of my being wanted to be his completely.

"Me too," I said softly against his lips.

I heard him draw a long breath. A warm, heady feeling conquered me as he kissed me deeply. He sucked my tongue hungrily as his right hand kneaded my left breast.

"Have you ever thought of us this way, sweetheart?" he asked, his voice husky, as his thumb played with my puckered nipple through the layers of my clothes, making my body beg for more.

"Yes. But I didn't know this would feel this good," I whispered, pressing myself closer to him."Have you?"

"All the time. I have fantasized about us so much and I want to make all my fantasies a reality today," he said and picked me up in his arms again. His heated gaze spoke of his secret desires as he whispered in my ears. "I have a cosy, warm bed upstairs, which is necessary to complete the picture. Shall we?"

I nodded and hugged him tight as he carried me up the stairs, feeling breathless and excited. I hid my face in his chest, enjoying the rhythm of his heart that was in perfect sync with my own.

25
Navneet

I ached to see her, touch her and lose myself in her warmth as I made her sit on my bed.

"I want to see you," I told her, and she lowered her gaze. I loved the blush that crept onto her face.

With trembling fingers, I lifted her top and removed it. My heart skipped a beat when I saw her cleavage covered with a lacy bra. Her nipples had pebbled and I leaned to kiss them one after the other. She shuddered as I bit her right nipple lightly. I unhooked her bra and peeled it off. With a sharply indrawn breath, she crossed her arms to hide them from my heated gaze.

Wordlessly, I moved her arm away and allowed my gaze to rove over her naked torso. I had never seen anything as enticing as her breasts. Round and full with pebbled nipples that begged to be licked, sucked and teased. I watched with fascination as they rose and fell rhythmically. Her breath quickened as I cupped her naked breasts reverently. They were soft and supple, just as I had imagined. Like I had wanted to do all along, I lowered my head and closed my mouth around a puckered nipple. She squirmed as I sucked, licked and nibbled it, and then repeated the same on her other breast. Her hands grabbed my hair as I continued to tease and caress her breasts. I had read somewhere that it was possible to make a woman come, just by caressing her breasts. I wanted to test it. I wanted to pleasure her in every way possible before the day ended. And also, pleasuring her was making my body grow harder. I felt like I could do this for hours. I continued to pleasure her and it wasn't long before she arched into me, begging for more. Pressing my face into her cleavage, I kneaded her breasts, over and over, alternating it with playing with her nipples. Before long, she screamed my name, shuddered and came apart in my arms. Wow! So, the theory was true.

"What are you doing to me?" she asked, her eyes dazed.

I kissed her hard on the lips and she kissed me back.

"This is so not fair," she complained, looking at my completely clothed body. As she watched, I took off my T-shirt. Aathira's eyes heated as her eyes roamed over my abs. All the hours I had spent developing and maintaining them felt fruitful for the first time. When she traced her fingers over my pectorals and then down to my abs, it was my turn to shudder.

She gazed into my eyes as she unbuckled my belt. And as I watched, she undid my jeans button before her fingers paused on my zipper. I hadn't expected my girl from the hills to be this bold. But the feel of her fingers on my groin made my erection grow hard. She pushed down my pants and soon, I was standing before her dressed only in my boxers. She cupped me there and I groaned. I had to distract her or it would have been all over even before it started.

I pulled her up and made her stand in front of the dressing table mirror. As she watched us in the mirror, I proceeded to undress her completely. I loved how she blushed when she saw me knead her breasts and run my hands all over her lush body. When our eyes met in the mirror, she hid her face with her hands and then turned to hide her face in my chest. A groan escaped my lips when her soft breasts crushed against my chest. It was my undoing when I got the first glimpse of her perfect high and tight derriere in the mirror.

I cupped her bottom, squeezed it and whispered in her ears, "I think, I want to marry these two."

She punched my chest. "You are a pervert!"

With a grin, I removed my boxers, lifted her in my arms and fell into the bed, her warm body covering mine. It took every bit of my willpower to not flip her over and drive into her. Instead, I pulled open the drawer next to the bed, took out a condom and donned it as she watched.

"I am all yours. Ride me, my queen," I said, guiding her to straddle me. Her eyes widened.

"I don't know. This is my first time," she said and blushed heavily.

"Your body will know exactly how...," I touched her core with my hard member. It took her a few seconds, but soon her warmth enveloped me and she was riding me like there was no tomorrow. I kneaded her breast and twisted her nipples as she bounced up and down, again and again. It was bliss like none other to see her ride her orgasm as she screamed my name. She collapsed over me, her contractions squeezing me in the most pleasurable way, almost tipping me over the edge of ecstasy. I flipped her over and pumped into her over and over until my world burst with colours. We stayed that way, our bodies sated, our souls revelling in the enchantment created by our togetherness.

I reached for her again a while later for a repeat performance.

It was around three in the afternoon that we finally got out of bed. Not because we had talked, explored and made love enough but because our stomachs had started to protest loudly, making the most alarming sounds. Aathira stepped out from the bed saying she would dish up something from the kitchen.

"Hey, do you think your boyfriend is that thoughtless? I had the cook prepare a complete meal for us before I dismissed him today morning. We have all your favourite Karnataka dishes waiting for you in the dining room. We may have to warm the food though given how late it is already."

"I am impressed," she said as she picked up her clothes from the bedroom couch.

"Don't dress yet. I am not done yet," I said, letting my eyes roam all over her beautiful body.

"Come on. I can't possibly eat in my birthday suit! Also, I feel sticky-sticky all over. Maybe I should take a shower."

"Go ahead and take a bath. I will find something for you to wear," I said and lust gripped me again as she stepped into the adjoining bathroom. When she was about to close the door, I dashed to her and whispered, "I don't want to leave you alone in there. Let's do it together."

Aathira protested once but quickly gave in. The result was that we ate our lunch at four in the evening dressed in identical blue T-shirts. The cook had made vegetable pulav, curd rice, *akki roti*, *poori* with potato *bhaji* and *sheera* for dessert.

"Yum. These are all my favourite dishes indeed. I fell in love with them after coming to Bangalore. But how did you know?" Aathira asked.

"Thank Trisha. She gave me a long list of things you love," I said. Trisha had listed almost all the things that

Aathira loved eating after moving to Bangalore.

Vishal called around the time we finished lunch. I put him on speaker phone as I was busy cuddling Aathira. "I know you asked not to call as you plan to spend time with Aathira. But I have to remind you that you have to get admitted to the hospital today before seven, okay?"

That meant I should leave in another hour considering how heavy Bangalore traffic was in the evenings.

Aathira looked distressed when she heard it. I gathered her in my arms once I disconnected the phone.

"I will never forget today. And this is just the beginning of a long life of our togetherness, sweetheart. I need your courage now. Promise me, you will be my biggest support system once I wake up after the surgery," I said, cupping her face.

She kissed my lips and said softly, "I promise." Yet, the next moment she burst into tears.

I kissed away her tears and hugged her tightly.

"I want to come with you," she said.

"You can. I want you to come with me," I said, and together we returned to the bedroom to pack my bag. I could ask my driver to drop her back after the visiting hours were over.

When I looked at her running around gathering stuff that she thought I would need, I felt a pang in my heart.

I was going to be an invalid for the next few weeks in the literal sense. I wouldn't be able to have fun with her or make love to her till I recovered.

Now that I knew what heaven tasted like, everything else felt like hell. So, I spent the next precious hour making memories that would energise me for the impending period of inaction, laughing with her, kissing her and making every second matter.

When we were in the car, Vishal called again. He sounded panic-stricken.

"Navneet, you have to hurry. Ammamma's vitals have dropped. The doctors want to bring forward the transplant and want to do it today as they worry she may not last the night otherwise."

"I will be there in half an hour. Ask the doctors to prepare for the operation," I said and Aathira clutched my arm. Her eyes were wide with concern.

"All is well, okay? Just relax," I said.

"Ammamma will be fine. And you will be fine too," she told me. Though it sounded as if she were saying those words aloud to convince herself, her words continued to echo in my mind all the way to the hospital.

26

Aathira

Hospitals made me nervous. That was the main reason that I didn't write the medical entrance test after the twelfth board exams, even though I had been one of the state toppers in biology. My biology teacher was disappointed to learn that I had opted for engineering instead. I could never see myself as a doctor, brave enough to save people.

Like everyone else in the waiting room, I was trying to stay calm. No one was talking. Except for Navneet's brother Naveen, Arya Ma'am and his mother, everyone else I knew from the Sreepuram family was there. Naveen and the others had been unreachable on the phone. The temple they had been visiting was located in a remote village with a bad network coverage.

After a day of utter bliss, I hadn't expected to face this. The look on Navneet's face as his gurney was being rolled into the operation theatre still haunted me. He was smiling at us but somehow it didn't reach his eyes. When he squeezed my hands, I saw something that I had never seen on his face. Fear. Had I projected my fears on him? I felt terrible. I patted his hands and pasted a brave smile on my face even though on the inside I was as nervous as a cat on hot bricks.

Shreya sat beside me and she encouraged me to try a novel she had picked up from a nearby bookshop. Though I took the book from her, I couldn't read. I kept thinking of the happy moments I had spent with Navneet, his words, his actions and his promises. I kept looking at the promise ring he had given me.

Vishal and Arjun were deep in discussion at one corner of the waiting room. No one talked. Some of the older women tried to sleep, while the younger women stayed awake. They tried to engage me in small talk but their questions didn't even register at times because I was too distracted by the thoughts roaring in my head. They stopped trying after a few failed attempts.

Naveen and the rest of the family rushed in a few hours into the surgery. They all appeared anxious. Naveen looked a bit angry too.

"What happened? Why was the operation hurried? And why wasn't I informed?" Naveen asked Vishal immediately upon entering the waiting room.

"They had to do it because Ammamma's vitals were dropping. And we tried calling you. Your phone was out of coverage area."

"This shouldn't have happened. Today is not a good day. The stars are not in his favour," muttered Naveen as he slumped onto one of the chairs near me.

His words fell like molten lava into my ears and immediately all the anxiety that I had been trying to curb, came out in a rush. I felt dizzy and held onto my chair handle to support my keeling body.

"Relax. Everything is under control. I am getting updates from inside the theatre from one of the stand by nurses. The surgery is proceeding according to schedule and both,

Ammamma and Navneet, are stable," said Vishal.

Just then his mobile pinged and he tapped the screen to read it. He blanched and I knew something terrible had happened. I could just feel it.

"What is it?" asked Naveen, who had also noticed Vishal's pale face.

"It's...it's Navneet. He suffered a cardiac arrest and they are trying to revive him right now. They suspect it was an allergic reaction to one of the components used in the anaesthesia," Vishal said in a very low voice. But I heard every single word.

Cardiac arrest? No. I might have heard it wrong.

One look at the grief-stricken faces of Naveen and Vishal confirmed that I had heard it right. Vishal was explaining the details as further texts arrived.

My heart raced and sweat broke out on my forehead. A chill enveloped me and my whole body started trembling. I felt dizzy, my hands felt numb and refused to move. Before I could comprehend what was happening darkness enveloped me.

When I became conscious, I was in the emergency room and Ananya was sitting beside my bed. On realizing that I had regained consciousness, she held my hand and patted it.

"Navneet is okay. They managed to revive him. They found out what exactly was causing the reaction and administered the antidote. So, the operation is proceeding without any delay. It is almost over, according to Vishal," said Ananya.

"Thank God. Thank God," I murmured, holding onto her hands. She reached out to wipe my tears.

"Your hero will be back in no time. Don't let him miss you. The doctors gave you medicine to stop your panic attack and that put you to sleep. You have been unconscious for nearly an hour now," said Ananya.

"I am so sorry. I just added to your troubles."

"You did nothing of the sort. Your reaction was expected. I just texted the others. They were worried about you. Now rest."

I squeezed Ananya's hand and looked away trying to compose myself.

I don't know what I would have done if something had happened to Navneet.

Arya Ma'am came into the ER just then and sat next to me.

"Are you okay now?" she asked, tucking an out-of-place strand of hair behind my ears.

"Yes," I said feeling embarrassed.

Just then Ananya gave a short whoop and spoke to us, "Vishal just texted. The operation was successful. According to the doctors, both Ammamma and Navneet are stable."

We all heaved a sigh of relief and smiles lit up all our faces. I sent a quick prayer of gratitude to the heavens.

Kishore came in just then with Shreya. I sat up and greeted them.

"Naveen has put me in charge to drop you home. So, once Ammamma and Navneet get transferred to the ICU, we will leave, okay?"

Arjun, Shalini and Vishal came into the ER next and I started to feel terrible. Because of me, they had to come to the ground floor ER room. I couldn't even look at their faces.

"How is the latest member of the Sreepuram family?" asked Vishal as he came and stood next to my bed, and I felt immensely grateful.

They were already treating me as a part of the family.

"Do you all really want a troublesome new member like me?" I asked, looking at their faces.

"Oh, you didn't know? Being troublesome is a must-have trait for every member of the Sreepuram family," said Ananya.

"Silly girl… You don't have any choice in that matter. We can't have our crybaby become Devdas yet another time. Navneet always gets what he wants. And it is clear as day that he wants you now," said Kishore.

"Yes. And with that fainting spell, you proved to us how much Navneet matters to you. So, it is time we officially welcomed you into the family. Ananya, will you do the honours?" asked Vishal, and Ananya immediately said yes and began tapping on her phone. Then she handed me my phone.

"Welcome to our crazy family, Aathira. I feel sorry for you. Now, you are stuck with us. You will have to put up with us your entire life," she said with a wide smile on her face.

I took the phone wondering what she meant. A WhatsApp notification popped up on my screen.

Ananya has added you to the Sreepuram Family group.

Welcome messages from almost every member of the family started pouring in.

Tears pricked the back of my eyes, and soon enough my eyes were brimming with tears.

"Oh, God! Our crybaby is going to marry another crybaby," exclaimed Kishore. Shreya punched him hard in the arms.

Embarrassed, I quickly swiped away my tears.

Vishal said aloud, "Ignore my big bro. He can't help being a bully. We will teach you how to deal with him. So, don't worry."

Gratitude flooded me. Now all I could do was wait. Wait for my dear dog- whisperer to wake up.

I couldn't wait to see him smile at me. I couldn't wait to hug and kiss him.

But perhaps God wasn't done testing us yet. Around seven in the morning, Ammamma regained consciousness. But Navneet didn't. When consulted, the doctors said it sometimes happened that way because of the complications that could have arisen due to the cardiac arrest.

"All his vitals are normal. So, don't worry. He should wake up within a few hours," said Dr Bhatt, when he came out of the ICU after checking his patients.

Eight hours passed, then twenty-four hours passed and still, Navneet didn't wake up. The doctors now feared he had slipped into a coma.

Every second from then on, I begged the creator to stop testing us. Hadn't he tested us enough? All I had wished was to be near Navneet. To love him and to be loved by him. I didn't want anything else. But God wasn't listening to my pleas.

Ammamma who was transferred to a recovery room now had gotten better enough to talk. She was furious when she realised that she had undergone a transplant. Then she demanded to meet her donor. When nobody gave her the details, she demanded to see Navneet. I was sure she suspected Navneet was the donor because of his absence in the crowd around her.

The doctors had asked us to keep her stress-free and hence no one told her the truth.

"He left on an urgent business trip, Ammamma," said Vishal, when she stubbornly demanded to see Navneet.

But Ammamma was hearing none of it. She glared at him.

"Don't expect me to believe that. He wouldn't leave before speaking to me," she said, suspecting the worst.

So, I had to step in.

"That's why I am here, Ammamma. He left only after your operation was over. It was an emergency and he will be back in a few days. He left me in charge to take care of you. See, he gave me this," I said, showing her the promise ring Navneet had given me.

She sighed with relief on hearing my words. Holding my hand, she admired the ring.

"Okay. Tell him to video call me when he calls next," she said, giving me a wan smile.

"I will. Now please go back to sleep," I said, and to my relief, she complied.

Kishore patted my back when I came out of the room.

"Thank you for doing that. We were at our wit's end making up excuses."

I ran out into the hospital garden to gather myself. It was easy to lie to calm her down. I wished someone would lie to me that Navneet was back. I hadn't slept for even a wink for the last two nights. Whenever I tried to close my eyes, the possibility of something terrible happening to Navneet would shake me up, pushing away every likelihood of falling asleep.

Just then, I heard temple bells from the tiny Ganesha temple in front of the hospital. On an impulse, with trembling steps, I walked into the temple. I sat in the outer chamber facing the deity and prayed. The evening *puja* was going on, so the inner chamber was closed. I don't know how long I stayed that way, but I had never prayed as fervently as that before for anything. The continuous tolling of the bells, a while later, made me look up. The priest had opened the inner chamber after the *puja* and the devotees were crowding in front of the chamber to get a proper glimpse of the deity. Lit by the light of a hundred small lamps, the Ganesha idol made out of white marble, looked resplendent. I felt like he was looking at me with his benevolent eyes. Peace flooded through me and just like that, I knew that Navneet was going to be fine.

As if to prove my conviction right, my mobile started buzzing inside my jeans pocket. It was Kishore.

"Where are you, kid? Your boy woke up. He is demanding to see you."

On hearing his words, I burst into tears. I thanked him profusely between sobs even as he kept asking where I was, whether he should come to pick me up and generally lamenting about how terrible a crybaby I was. I bowed to Ganesha, slipped a five hundred rupee note into the *hundi* there and dashed out of the temple with a grateful heart.

After keeping all of us on our toes for three straight days, my sweetheart had finally woken up. I couldn't wait to see him.

27

Navneet

When I opened my eyes, happy faces surrounded me. Each person welcomed me back in their own way.

"Finally, you are up. This is the longest you have slept," said my mother.

Simple words. Yet, each word carried a lot of emotions.

"Ammamma...?" I asked, clutching Naveen's arm.

"She is fine. She is waiting to see you."

Relief flooded me. And the next moment, longing filled me. I looked around to see that one face, my anchor, my love. My heart sank. She wasn't around.

"Aathira... where is she?"

"She stepped out to take a stroll in the garden. She has not left the hospital for days," said Ananya.

"Days?"

That one word told me I had lost days. And that perhaps these people had been worried sick about me while I slept.

"How long was I unconscious?" I asked, searching Naveen's face.

"Three days," he replied.

Three days? Before the operation, the doctor had said I would regain my consciousness once they stopped giving me the anaesthesia and gave me the antidote to wake up. What had caused the delay? It just felt as if I was waking up from a long sleep. My body felt sore as if it had been run over by a truck and my mind was hazy. There were multiple tubes connected to my body. Maybe there was more to the story.

"Why? What happened?" I asked Vishal who was standing on the other side of the bed.

"We will talk about it all once you regain your energy. Now we will give you some alone time with your sweetheart," said Vishal, pointing at Aathira who had just entered the recovery room. She was panting as if she had run all the way here. Her face lit up with a happy smile, warming up my whole being.

I lifted my arms, inviting her into my arms. She dashed to my side, as the room slowly emptied. As soon as we were alone, she laughed heartily and peppered my face with kisses.

She looked sleep deprived and her eyes were red from crying. I felt guilty. Even though I had vowed to never make her cry, I had inadvertently managed to do just that.

"Promise me, you will never scare me like this again," she said softly, holding my hand.

"I promise. And keep your promise to be by my side from now on," I said, holding her gaze.

"At this rate, I will be kicked out from your company in the first month itself, Mr CEO. I haven't attended the training since Monday," she said, her eyes twinkling.

"Don't worry about that. No one will dare to kick you out of QIS. I can't spend my days here without you near me," I said.

We talked for a few more minutes before the nurse came in to check my vitals and inject the next dose of my medicine.

Soon, I slipped back into a deep sleep. When I opened my eyes again, the first face I saw was that of Aathira. She was sitting on the couch near the door reading a book. My mother was engaged in peeling oranges and as I watched, she offered them to Aathira who politely refused them.

"You should eat properly. You can't give from an empty cup. You need your energy if you want to be by his side. To look after an invalid will take up a lot of energy."

"I am not hungry, Amma. I ate dinner just a few minutes ago."

"Why don't you rest for a while then? He will probably sleep through the night. Shall I ask Naveen to drop you off? Come back in the morning. I will stay here."

"No, Amma. Vishal said your BP is still high. You should go home and rest. I am okay. I will stay here," said Aathira.

My heart squeezed watching the two women in my life trying to watch out for each other. I liked that she was already addressing my mother as Amma. I decided it was time to let them know that I was wide awake. It was time I stopped being selfish.

"Ladies, go home and rest. I am craving some male company tonight," I said just as I saw Arjun walk in with Ananya.

"I will consider it an honour if your lordship will allow me to be your servant for tonight," said Arjun, looking at me.

"And I can be your servant's servant," said Ananya.

"I would have loved that but I don't think they allow two people in here with the patient," I said, smiling at them.

"Fine then. Don't tire my hubby by acting like a baby all night," warned Ananya. Then she turned to the two women and offered to drop them both at their respective homes.

Amma and Aathira left after making sure I was okay.

"Don't make her wait for long. You should marry her soon," said Arjun as he sat near my bed.

"I want nothing else. If I can marry her today, I will do it. I can't wait to make her mine."

He gave me a loaded look and then grinned widely.

"I think it will be prudent to wait for a few months. Your libido will take a while to return after an operation like this," he said.

I chuckled. That just didn't seem to apply to me. Whenever she came near, she made me go hard. That part of my body didn't listen to anyone or anything when it came to her. I didn't think anything had changed. Of course, now I was under the influence of various antibiotics and other drugs and my entire body ached.

"I think I might be an exception," I told him. He sniggered.

The eagerness to bind me and Aathira together was so strong among everyone in the family that I didn't even need to lift a single finger or utter a single word to set the marriage proposal in motion.

Ammamma, who by now knew the truth about the transplant and her donor, was prompt enough to send a team to Aathira's home with the proposal even though she was mad that I had taken such a huge risk. Before I left the hospital, we were officially engaged.

The next few weeks flew past like a pleasant breeze. To my happiness, Aathira remained by my side 24/7 and played a major role in my recovery. When the heart and mind are happy, the body heals super fast.

By the end of the first week itself, I felt almost normal. Well enough to sit up and even stand or take a few steps albeit with help. Aathira was my favourite crutch. The doctors had advised me to do breathing exercises to clear my lungs. IVs and other tubes were soon removed and I was pronounced healthy enough to be discharged.

The pain from the incision was negligible by the end of the second week and I didn't need the prescription pills anymore. I started going for short walks in the terrace garden with Aathira. My best hours were those that we spent there watching the night sky while lying on the lounge chairs near the pool. The more we talked, the closer we became.

Regular check-ups were due weekly and there was round-the-clock monitoring by Arjun and Vishal who were taking turns to care for Ammamma and me. Food was the only downside as I couldn't eat anything that would put a strain on my regenerating liver.

By the end of the fifth week, I felt healthy enough to roam around Bangalore with Aathira. We took the metro to travel to some of the most touristy places. I returned to the company briefly too and everything was back to where it belonged.

Most importantly, Ammamma was back with us, hale and hearty. And that was all that mattered. My girl from the hills was now a part of my life. She had become close to all my cousins and their spouses during our time at the hospital. To my surprise, Kishore had declared himself as her big brother and told everyone that anyone messing up with her would have to go through him. With the big bully becoming her Godfather, Aathira soon became the family pet.

I came to know that she had acquired a new nickname though. Crybaby. She had gladly inherited my old nickname.

I watched her fondly as she came into the room with a smoothie. You wouldn't find a happier man than me in the entire universe now because we were officially stepping into our forever at the end of next month.

28

Aathira

If someone told me a few months ago that I'd be marrying a handsome billionaire who loved me like crazy, I would have run in the opposite direction. The person saying so had to be insane, right?

The past months had been inexplicable and my life had become the stuff fairytales were made of.

Once Navneet was declared fit to travel, his first trip was to my home in Wayanad to officially ask for my hand in marriage. The proposal had been swiftly accepted as Navneet's family members had already visited my home multiple times before that. An engagement ceremony was held the very next day.

It was a different matter that even before the engagement, we were together 24/7. He had appointed me as his executive assistant which meant I had to be at his beck and call at all times. And after the engagement, our romance became the hottest topic in QIS.

I married my dog-whisperer in a grand but private ceremony held in Bangalore with about 300 guests in attendance. The red *Banarasi* silk sari Navneet had chosen for me made me feel beautiful and elegant like a medieval princess. Navneet had dressed in the traditional white *mundu* and white button-down silk shirt. And trust me, he looked as gorgeous in that typical Mallu look as he did in any custom-made suit.

My bridesmaids, Sneha, Trisha and Riddhi dressed in golden colours. Navneet's gang of brothers were also dressed uniformly in white traditional *mundu* and maroon silk shirts. The Sreepuram women had come attired in their best.

Once my prince charming tied the *thali*, the sacred marriage chain, around my neck, he kissed me on the cheek soon after, making everyone in the audience cheer and clap. During lunch, he insisted I feed him the first dollop of the wedding feast and I complied. Both videos went viral on social media courtesy of the Star Quartet.

It took some time for my bewildered parents to actually believe that their daughter had indeed got married without them even lifting a finger to make it happen. Navneet demanded dowry though. My little mutt Sheru! Thus my lucky devil acquired a new slave who took him on long walks and treated him like the very incarnation of God. Navneet made him a special home in the terrace garden and even appointed a caretaker.

During the hectic weeks before our wedding, all I'd looked forward was to exploring a new place and spending time with my dear husband during our honeymoon. But as was the trend in my life currently, I got more than what I wished for.

Sunrises in the hills were magical and the magic was entirely orchestrated by the creator. What I was currently witnessing was equally mesmerizing but this picturesque view had a human element involved in its creation.

Right before my eyes, hundreds of rainbow-coloured hot air balloons floated in the morning sky as the majestic sun experimented with hues of red and yellow. As our balloon soared into the sky, I took in the breathtaking beauty of Cappadocia, an ancient district in east-central Anatolia, situated on the rugged plateau north of the Taurus Mountains, in the centre of present-day Turkey.

Navneet hugged me tightly from behind and pressed a kiss on my cheek. It felt as if we were inside a fairytale. All around us, we could see honeycombed hills, towering boulders, cave dwellings, remarkable rock formations, and dramatic landscapes carved out from the soft volcanic rock, shaped by erosion into towers, cones, valleys and caves. It almost felt as if we were on another planet.

Was I experiencing magic or a miracle? I didn't know what to call it.

Ever since that evening with Navneet in the hills, my life was filled with thousands of tiny little miracles. If I were to write my own story, I don't know what I would call it. It was nothing like the usual rags to riches stories. Like Navneet often said, some passing fairy had sprinkled a very special magical dust on us that day in the hills and tied our hearts together with an invisible thread.

I sighed happily as Navneet turned me to him to press a gentle kiss on my lips.

"This calls for a selfie, don't you agree?" he asked as he clicked a photo of us smiling, our cheeks pressed together, the scenic background of Cappadocia adding its splendour to the picture.

I felt grateful for that moment, for the beauty around me and for the man who made me fall in love with him over and over again, every single day.

It was a blessing to be married to the one I loved, a blessing to be loved so ardently and to be cherished by Navneet like I was the most important person for him in the world. But the greatest blessing I felt was to be a part of the loving Sreepuram family. Commitment and love bonded us together and I knew that they would always have my back. I could now understand why they were that way. The Sreepuram family tree had a strong root in the form of Ammamma who had anchored the family firmly. Now that she was back to normal, fun times were back in the family.

Our marriage was held in Bangalore to make sure Ammamma got enough time to recuperate. The doctors had given a go-ahead for Navneet after tests revealed that eighty per cent of his liver had regenerated. Though there were still restrictions on alcohol, red meat and other fatty foods, Navneet was happy with his current diet plan. He consumed what he called his 'happy' food without much fuss. To give him company I was following the same diet. The result was that I felt more energetic and light every day, making me wonder if all the tasty food that we consumed was indeed the reason why we fell sick easily.

In Capadoccia, we had initially survived mainly on salads. Then our tour guide introduced us to traditional Turkish vegetarian food. On his advice, we tried the mixed mezze plate which had veggies stuffed inside grape leaves, vegetable stews, curd-based dips and fritters. It was served alongside whole bread. We also tried the Gozleme, a Turkish version of our stuffed parathas and also Borek, another stuffed bread.

Once we returned to the quaint cave-side hotel where we were staying, I opened Whatsapp and sent our pics to my Star Quartet. Navneet was doing the same in the family group.

Replies popped up one after the other.

The first one to respond was Sneha.

Sneha: That looks so dreamy. I am so jealous.

Trisha: You guys woke up so early? Or didn't you sleep at all?

Riddhi: Look at their eyes. It's clearly the latter.

Me: Shut up. We slept early yesterday!

Riddhi: Yes. We totally believe that.

Me: *3 winking emojis*

Trisha: When are we getting a tell-all episode?

Me: Never.

Riddhi: Traitor. You promised.

Sneha: Leave her alone, girls. Some things should remain private. *blushing emojis*

Riddhi immediately started a group video call and I joined.

"Promises are meant to be kept especially between best friends," Riddhi said in a low voice on seeing Navneet talking on the phone on the balcony.

"Don't think we will allow you to walk scot-free. Be kind to your noob friends," said Trisha.

"Tell them if you want. I don't even want to think about it. Gross," said Sneha.

"There is nothing gross about it, Sneha. I guess you will soon be singing a different tune once your Mr Perfect comes along," I said, and Riddhi and Trisha chuckled.

"Kissing and all is okay. But what comes after that is gross," said Sneha.

How could I convince this girl that what came after that was even more glorious than a kiss? That a kiss was just the tip of a delicious iceberg? That there were a thousand ways to find pleasure in the company of the right lover?

"Okay, the others can wait. I promise I will tell you exactly what awaits you on the marriage bed in detail because I feel you really need it," I said to Sneha and the other two pouted.

Navneet came into the room just then and I quickly said goodbye to the girls and ended the call.

With a smile, he walked toward the smart TV in the room, connected his phone to it and clicked open his music playlist. It was during my time caring for him that I discovered that he used to be a dancing star in college. And from then on, dancing for him and with him had become the prelude to lovemaking.

Navneet extended his right hand towards me and I kept mine on his. Gathering me in his arms, he kissed me deeply and like always, I responded by pouring my soul into our kiss.

Making me sway to '*All of Me*' by John Legend, he pressed his body tightly against me, ground his hips against mine and stroked my arms, legs, neck and back, turning me on within minutes. By the time the song ended, we were both equally aroused and fell into bed in a tangled mess of limbs. Soon, I was screaming his name as he thrust into me repeatedly, creating our own little heaven on earth.

More than an act of pleasure, I loved how connected and comfortable he made me feel when he made love to me, every single time. Like Sneha, I had always thought sex was gross, but Navneet had made me think and feel differently. Often, the foreplay would become breathtaking to the point where I would feel I couldn't take it anymore. And I especially cherished the moments when it felt as if I had become a part of him. When I wouldn't know where he began and where I ended.

It was evident in the way we reached for each other a while later, in the passion that ruled us that night and in our cuddles the next morning that we would never get enough of each other.

This random girl from the hills had found home inside her dog whisperer's heart and had become his heartbeat. In return, he had become her breath, her hero and her forever.

— The End

Author's Note

Dear Reader,

Thank you for choosing to read this book. I really appreciate it.

I hope you enjoyed reading it as much as I enjoyed creating it.

Reviews matter to any book. If you liked the book, please leave a review on Amazon or Goodreads.

Word of mouth works wonders too. Please tell your other reader friends about this book.

If you wish to tell me how you liked the book, contact me on social media.

You can find me active on :

Instagram: @authorpreethi

Twitter: @preethivenu

Or

Email me: authorpreethi@gmail.com

Hoping to hear from you,

Regards,

Preethi Venugopala

This is the final book in the Sreepuram series and I am so thrilled to finally present it to you all.

Every book in the Sreepuram series has made me grow differently. Be it as a writer or as a person. I loved creating this family with a loving grandmother. My grandmothers were wise and loving and I thank them for making me believe in the strength of family, and loving relationships and also for feeding me with yummy food throughout my childhood. Arundhati Mukundan resembles my own Ammamma a lot. I lost her while I was in high school and I still miss her.

A writer can never write a book without a loving environment and I am thankful to my family, especially my son Akshaj and my husband Venugopala for providing me with just that.

As always, I thank my dear friend Aathira for being my sounding board. This book is in a way, a tribute to our friendship. Right from the moment I named the female lead after her, I have shared crucial twists and turns in the story with her. She was my first beta reader and I am so thankful that she loved it.

I received a lot of help from my friends in the medical field Dr Praveen and Dr Roshan Radhakrishnan for writing details about liver transplant. I am so thankful for all the help I received from them. If there are any errors, it is entirely my fault.

My editor Nikita was fully supportive even as I failed to deliver the manuscript on time due to my hectic work schedule. She took pains to complete this project on time to help me keep my promise to my readers. Thank you dear for your support and amazing work.

I thank you, dear reader, for choosing to cheer the Sreepuram gang with every book. I think I might write stories of the Star Quartet girls next.

And dear God, thank you for the stories you send my way. Thank you for infusing me with creativity.

— **Preethi Venugopala.**

PREETHI VENUGOPALA has always loved books. Her late father introduced her to the world of fiction. She is a certified Potterhead, a Gryffindor to the core, and a big fan of JK Rowling. She is in the process of turning her son into a Potterhead as well with notable progress to date.

She is also an educator who teaches at a Caribbean University. Her latest pet project is her creative writing school, 'Cosmic Creativity Hub'

She has a bachelor's degree in civil engineering and a master's degree in English literature. She is also an alumnus of the famed 'Anita's Attic', a creative writing school by author Anita Nair.

Blurbs of Novels by Preethi Venugopala

Book 1: The Girl at the Wedding

A Sweet Romance Novella about Arranged Marriages, Family and Love.

Kishore is home on vacation after three years. To his horror, his family is determined to get him married this time. He creates the perfect plan to escape the matchmaking attempts of his family. Just when he thought he had everything under control, a girl from his past literally crashes into his life and turns his life upside down. Within a day, he is ready to sacrifice his bachelorhood entranced by the girl he meets at his friend's wedding.

One misstep and he acquires a rival. His own cousin, Abhishek.

What can he do to win back the love of his life?

Shreya can't believe that the handsome young man she is slowly falling in love with is the bully she hated in school. He has transformed in every possible way. She likes everything about him. But then something happens that prompts her to make a rash decision.

Would this one decision ruin her chances of finding true love?

Or would she have the courage to fight for love?

Book 2: Without You

Blurb:

Dr Arjun enters Ananya's life like a whirlwind, bringing with him the spirit of young love.

Does the path of true love ever run smooth?

Circumstances force them apart even though they were irrevocably in love. She becomes a victim of depression. When everything fails to return her to normalcy, help arrives from an unexpected source.

Will she ever find happiness again?

Will time allow her heart to heal and forget Arjun?

What indeed is true love?

What is that strange secret that locks all the circumstances together?

Travel with Ananya to the picturesque Sreepuram, face the chaos of Bengaluru, and relish the warmth of magical Dubai in this heartwarming tale of love, betrayal, friendship, and miracles.

Book 3: His Sunshine Girl

Can two damaged souls heal each other?

Shalini is dusky and has faced body shaming throughout her life because of it. She has gone through a lot in her life, including a failed marriage and divorce, and is at a crossroads when the story begins.

She arrives in Sreepuram as the live-in literary assistant to Arundhati Mukundan, an eminent author.

Dr Vishal, Arundhati's grandson and a paediatrician, has seen love and loss at close quarters.

When they meet in Sreepuram, it is a reunion of two childhood friends who were once inseparable.

Will their friendship help them heal?

Isn't friendship turning into love the most beautiful thing on earth?

Would fate allow that to happen or would it play its devious role again?

This is a standalone sequel to the best seller 'Without You'. You can read this even if you haven't read 'Without You.'

This story picks up from where 'Without You' ended.

Look out for some of your favourite characters from 'Without You' taking on significant roles in this story.

Book 4: What the Stars Knew

Are our destinies written in the stars?

Meet two starcrossed lovers. Naveen and Arya.

One is a techie turned famed Vedic astrologer, and a millionaire Youtube Celebrity. The other is an ex-techie building her life back up from ashes.

Arya: Could someone shatter your heart into a million pieces with a single word?

Once, someone did that to me. I'd vowed to forget Naveen, became somebody else's forever only to realize that forevers don't exist.

I didn't realize the power of our shared memories until he returned.

And now, I can't stop myself from rushing into his arms.

I can't stop myself from falling for him all over again.

But Naveen is not the boy I once knew.

He now speaks of what the stars know, and unforeseen destinies.

All I care about is whether we have a future together.

Naveen: I won't survive if I lose Arya again.

The memory of us has hounded me for years.

I regret the moment I left her years ago.

I believed I could forget her.

But time has proven otherwise.

Her dark eyes still bewitch me, luring me into their depths.

But the stars tell me, she is not mine to cherish.

For the first time, I want to challenge them.

I want her to be mine forever.

What do the stars know?

What is written in the destiny of Naveen and Arya?

P.S: Though this is part of the Sreepuram series, this story works as a standalone as well. You don't have to read the other books in the series to enjoy this book.

Book 1: A Royal Affair

Blurb:

A British commoner in love with an Indian Prince

When Jane Worthington, a reporter with a London-based entertainment channel, comes to India she is sure of two things.

Firstly, she would find Daniel Worthington, the lost twin of her beloved Grandfather and fulfil his last wish.

Secondly, now that she was in India, she was not going to think about Prince Vijay Dev Varman, the scion of the erstwhile royal family of Sravanapura, the man who broke her heart years ago.

Two seemingly impossible tasks.

Vijay always believed he knew everything about himself and his family. But when Jane storms back into his life, secrets tumble out one after the other disturbing the very thread of discipline that had granted his life a semblance of sanity.

Jane cannot refuse Vijay's offer of help but every moment with him is torture because he is not the carefree youth she had once fallen in love with.

Will they succeed to find Daniel Worthington when every single trace of his existence seems to have been carefully wiped off by unseen hands?

Or will their quest reveal secrets that will make it impossible for them to even dream of a happily ever after?

A Suspense Novella about Second Chances in Love

Book 2: The Princess and the Superstar

A Princess in love with a Bollywood Superstar

Saketh Rao aka SR, India's latest Bollywood heartthrob, has bagged the role of a lifetime: to play Hari Varman, the doomed royal scion.

When he arrives at Sravanapura Palace with his director friend Rajeev Ratnam, little does he know that his life is about to change forever!

Princess Kritika is overjoyed that Saketh Rao will play the role of her ancestor. But when she comes face to face with the arrogant superstar she is determined to scuttle the project.

Fate, however, has different plans for them. The feisty couple is soon head over heels in love with each other.

As they uncover the secrets of Hari Varman's life, Saketh makes a discovery that can rip them apart and their new-found love.

Will the secrets and lies of the past deny them a future together?

Or will they overcome the obstacles to love?

Book 3: The Lost Princess

HOW FAR WOULD YOU GO TO PROTECT THE ONE YOU LOVE?

Ishaani, the newly crowned nightingale of the Indian music industry has it all: a dream career, a loving family and loyal friends. Yet, the man she has loved all her life will not warm up to her.

Rajeev, a hotshot movie director, has feelings for Ishaani. But, she is his sister's best friend and has been like another sibling to him. Yet, what can he do if he feels compelled to make her his own?

Then, Ishaani's life changes overnight. She is no longer a lowly commoner but a princess.

She has to make some tough decisions to protect the man she loves.

Her choices lead them both down a path filled with shocking revelations and devastating consequences.

Will true love prevail?

Or will the many twists of fate tear them apart?

Book 4: Love and Longing in Firefly Season

Rashi Ratnam, the newly minted design assistant of **billionaire fashion designer** Neel Mishra, is sceptical when she leaves on a field trip to Kerala with her temperamental boss.

It doesn't matter that she has been harbouring a crush on her gorgeous boss since forever.

The man intimidates her and is cold like ice.

Also, he hasn't still forgotten his ex-girlfriend.

At **Heaven's Cove**, the beautiful backwater island owned by Neel's grandparents, Rashi begins to see Neel in a new light. She also discovers his best-kept secrets.

It is the **firefly season**, and there is nothing that stops her from falling madly in love with Neel.

But **love** is not easy.

With Neel's jealous ex-girlfriend hovering around them stirring up troubles, life becomes strenuous.

Can they face the curve balls that fate throws at them?

Or will their love die a slow death?

But in the end, is the choice theirs to make?

Read this heartwarming contemporary love story of letting go and letting love in.

P.S: This book can also be read as a standalone romance. So, you can read this even if you haven't read the Sravanapura Royals series.

A Passionate Love Story with the Chennai Floods 2015 as Backdrop

On the outside, Tara leads a perfect life. A home of her own, a handsome husband, a doting son and a promising career as an author.

But inside, she is a wreck. Her marriage is a sham and she hasn't succeeded in forgetting her one true love, Manu, the man she had wronged. The man she had almost married.

Manu, now the senior editor with a science portal, firmly believes that he has left Tara where she belonged: in his past. But in reality, he hasn't forgotten anything. Not the love nor the hurt.

Their past and present collide when they accidentally meet in **Chennai.** The city has come to a standstill after facing the worst **flood** in a century. While nature is unleashing its fury on humans, they must make peace with their past.

Will they have the courage to do that?

Can they fight the attraction that still burns bright?

Or will the bunch of people they are with, teach them new life lessons?

What is the secret that is burning Tara from within?

When what you seek is seeking you...

Karan: It all started at a masquerade ball. I took one look at the girl dressed as **Cinderella** and fell **head over heels** in love.

I was not someone who believed in love.

Yet, within a few hours, she made me crave for things I never knew I wanted.

I began to equate her presence with happiness.

Like a warm breeze on that winter night, she thawed my frozen heart.

At midnight, she ran away without telling me who she really was. Just like Cinderella.

I was never the same again.

I couldn't forget her, but she came visiting only in my dreams.

No matter what, I was determined to find her.

Chandni: Karan was not someone I could even dream about.

I was a poor orphan, a nobody.

He was a billionaire, the hottest bachelor in India, coveted by rich women everywhere.

A dance: that was all he asked.

But while we danced, I gave him my heart, knowing that the magic would end once he realized my true identity.

I was nothing but a cheat.

Yet, the **magic** didn't end that night.

A bizarre twist of fate put me in his path again. I had to hide my secret, even though I wished to confess everything to him.

Was watching him from afar the only thing that was written in my destiny?

♥ **What would you do when you come face to face with your past?** ♥

Social media which is often a source of entertainment can be a source of great sorrow as well. Especially **alumni WhatsApp groups**, as not all memories are pleasant.

When Ajay, now an IAS officer, gets added into his **college** WhatsApp group, all his classmates welcome him warmly. Except for Jasmine.

Jasmine and Ajay were inseparable while in college. Their relationship had transitioned from being **best friends to lovers** over the duration of the engineering course. But then **fate** intervened, and they became estranged.

Five years of silence have created a **wall of sorrow** between them. Their interactions in the class WhatsApp group are nothing like what they once used to be. Every moment churns out more anguish and unpleasantness.

Jasmine is still living with the repercussions of what had happened in the **past**. Ajay's indifference throws her into despair.

What had caused their **separation**?

Is **love** still hiding underneath their public facades?

What **lies** are they concealing?

Other Works By The Author

Short Stories
A Christmas in London
My Red Knight
Kid's Books
Anya and the Spring Fairy
The Teddy who ran away
Learn Malayalam Alphabets through English